THE INVISIBLE HORSE

FRANCES HENDERSON

Stoddart

To Darcy,
Audrey, and Angelo

First published in 1991 by
Stoddart Publishing Co. Limited
34 Lesmill Road
Toronto, Canada
M3B 2T6

Canadian Cataloguing in Publication Data

Frances Henderson
Invisible horse

ISBN 0-7737-5426-1

I. Title.

PS8513.A45B9 1991 C813'.54 C89-090621-1
PR9199.3.G34B9 1991

Cover Design: Brant Cowie/ArtPlus Ltd.
Cover Illustration: Gordon Weber
Typesetting: Tony Gordon Ltd.

Printed in Canada

Contents

1

A Dream Come to Life

The slam of the screen door woke Kate. She heard Sam swishing away from the cabin through the long, dewy grass, then pushing through pine needles that plinked faintly like the teeth of a comb. Downstairs a fire crackled and Mum was moving pots on top of the woodstove. Birds were trilling all around the house, and a cicada was announcing a hot June day.

Behind all these noises, though, lay a deep, satisfying silence. There was none of the distant roar of motors that had sounded through all Kate's years in the city. This was the first morning of their new life in the country, and they were free to make the most of it, for Mum had decided there was no point in starting a new school two weeks before summer holidays — especially as Kate was due to start high school next fall. So a day of exploring stretched ahead of them, and typically, Sam had rushed out to start it. But before joining him, Kate rolled over and snuggled her face into the pillow to savour the last of her dream.

The great horse galloped magnificently, surging forward like a river in spring flood. His long, dappled neck was arched, and his white mane floated free. From under his tossing forelock he looked at her out of huge dark eyes that said, "My splendid power is all ours, yours and mine, to enjoy."

In the dream some enemy was dropping bombs on the log cabin under cover of darkness. But whenever a bomb whistled earthward, Kate galloped up and swatted it with her horse's tail, and it turned into a balloon and floated away.

The dream likewise drifted away into the outer reaches of Kate's mind, for the cinnamony smell of French raisin toast was rising with the wood smoke.

As she wriggled out of the sleeping bag, she heard the growl of a truck labouring up their gravel road, and Sam shouting, "The telephone men are here, and they've got a horse in their truck!"

Kate froze. Had they moved to a place where dreams came true?

"*What*?" called Mum.

"See for yourself," said Sam, stepping inside. "In the back of their truck there's a big drum of cable and a horse."

"I hope it doesn't mean they need a week to hook up the phone and in the meantime they're providing pony express service," said Mum. "Sam, would you keep an eye on this French toast while I go talk to them?"

Sam watched her stride briskly down the hill to greet the men in coveralls who were climbing out of the truck. He was very curious to see what they were going to do. But they seemed in no hurry to begin, and he was hungry. A gigantic can of maple syrup stood on the dresser that was to serve as their kitchen counter. To save the sizzling golden squares from a black death, he lifted them carefully into a bowl and poured a fragrant stream of syrup. It was impossible to pour only a little from a full can, so who could blame him if his toast swam in a deep golden pool?

He carried the bowl over to the window so he could watch the phone crew while he ate. This breakfast was the best he had ever tasted. Maybe it was the smoky maple syrup from up the road, or maybe it was because this was the first meal he had ever helped cook for himself over a fire of wood he had gathered.

Sam had been deeply angry last winter when his big sister did that really dumb thing that suddenly made their family different from other people's and changed their whole lives. But now it struck him that there might be a good side to it all, if he could figure it out.

"What are they doing with the horse?" asked Kate, climbing carefully backwards down the steep stairs from the loft.

"Nothing yet," said Sam.

She turned, and the sunlight bounced off her

wispy hair and dark glasses. "Is there anything to drink?"

"Apple juice," he answered, handing her a bottle from the window sill.

"I wonder if we could keep a horse," said Kate. "We've got plenty of grass."

"Why would we want a horse?" he asked.

"To ride, of course. And for company, and because they're beautiful."

"I don't see what good a horse would be to *you*," Sam objected. "You'd ride it off the edge of a cliff."

"It would stop for cliffs. Haven't you heard of horse sense? And it would *feel* beautiful."

They heard the horse whinny outside. "Let's go see what's happening," said Kate.

"You mean you want *me* to see. But we might as well," said Sam, for the men seemed to be starting to work. Maybe they would let him help. He led Kate down the steep, rough slope to the road, where the truck was parked. Their mother had gone with two of the men to the new telephone pole, far down at the edge of the swamp. In the hundred years since this road was built and telephones were invented, no lines had yet come as far as this property, for beyond them lay nothing but hunting preserve.

The tailgate of the pickup was down, a board was laid over it, and an old man in a blue cap and high rubber boots was holding a rope attached to a halter around the horse's head. "Come on, old girl," he said. With a clatter and a rumble, the animal picked its way down the board onto what would be their front lawn if they ever mowed it.

The horse had flecks of white in its brown coat and shaggy white hair over its heels.

"Why do you use a horse?" asked Sam.

"Because she gets the job done," said the man. "She can climb hills and wade through swamps where you couldn't take a truck. Never needs spare parts, either." He winked at Kate. Sam dropped her hand, feeling uncomfortable because the man hadn't realized winks were wasted on her.

"What's her name?" asked Kate.

"Betsy. And mine is Herb Benson."

"Pleased to meet you. I'm Kate and this is Sam. Can I pat her?"

"Ka-ate!" protested her brother.

"Sure you can, she's a quiet old lady," said Mr. Benson, adjusting a thick collar around the horse's neck.

Kate took a step in his direction. Sam saw there would be no stopping her until one of those big grey feet crushed her toes. With a sigh of exasperation, he took her hand and put it on the horse's shoulder. When her fingers touched the horse, it was like plugging a lamp into a socket. Not only her face but her whole body lit up, and she seemed to grow another inch. "Hello, Betsy," she said, in the tone she might use to a rock star she'd been dying to meet.

Sam stole a glance at Mr. Benson and was relieved to see him smiling at the attention his horse was getting. Sam smiled back, and swatted a black-fly on his cheek.

"How about buckling that breech-strap for me, son?" asked Mr. Benson.

Sam blinked. When he had pictured being allowed to help install the telephone, he had imagined sophisticated electronic gadgets, not worn, chocolate-coloured leather that smelled of old hay. This was really starting from the bottom. He fastened the buckle Mr. Benson pointed to, near the hind end of the horse.

"Is this right?" asked Sam.

The horse looked around at him with large, thoughtful eyes, as if she had something to say but was too polite to open her mouth. Mr. Benson replied, "Yes, that's okay. Isn't she a good-looking old thing for a grandmother?"

"She's had foals?" asked Kate.

"Three of them, but only one by a heavy horse like herself. The others are riding horses, like."

"Do you still have them?" Kate asked.

"I've got the youngest, the half-Belgian. She goes as a team with her mother at the fairs. And we've got the eight-year-old that my son used to ride, till he went out west. Why, are you looking for a horse to buy?" He peered at her sharply over the horse's neck, trying to read her expression through her dark glasses. Her face was almost buried in Betsy's neck, and she was sniffing it the way their father savoured a rare glass of brandy.

To Sam's horror, she said, "We might be. Are you selling one?"

7

"My son is pretty well settled in Calgary now, and he's got nowhere to keep a horse. If we got a good offer on the grey, we might part with him."

"How much?" she asked.

"I've turned down a thousand for his sister," said Mr. Benson.

"But she's half your team," said Kate. "Would the saddle horse be worth as much?"

"He's a fine horse. Keith won a lot of ribbons on him. And he's almost pure white, and everyone knows a white horse is good luck. Git up, Betsy, they're waiting for us down by the swamp." He shook the lines, and the horse leaned into the collar and pulled the big drum away.

"Why did you talk as if we were shopping for a horse?" Sam hissed at his sister. "When Mum hears, she'll be mad."

"I was only asking. Mum said we should learn all we can about life in the country, and that includes the price of livestock."

Before Sam could begin to make her see how she'd been embarrassing him, their mother called. "Sam, would you go and get some water so I can make coffee for the men? We'll need plenty to wash the dishes and clean the house, too."

The two big peanut butter pails swung furiously as Sam stomped down the road. Chores, chores, and Sam had to do nearly all of them himself. They had to find a better way of getting water than hiking through the long grass and reeds to Waddle Creek. In a day or two there was supposed to be an electric pump for the old well, but that was still a hundred metres from the house.

Sam passed the lilac and apple trees whose fragrant blooms had charmed their mother into buying the property when she first laid eyes on it. Now the lilac blossom was an ugly brown and the apple a plain green, and instead of their fresh spring scent, the air was laden with bloodthirsty blackflies. He broke to a run to get away from them. They clung to him until they ran slap into a posse of dragonflies, which filled the air above the stream like blue helicopters. Under their cover, Sam dipped his pails into the clear current and clapped the lids on. A frog hopped between his feet.

"Well, well, here comes the bucket brigade," said a voice out of the sky. Throwing his head back, Sam saw a man hanging by his belt from the top of a telephone pole. He watched in admiration as the skilled hands connected their isolated cabin to the city they had left. And steadily, at a walking pace, the cable that would put them in instant touch with the whole wired world was unwound from the great wooden drum by the horse plodding through the rough grass. The muscles on her broad backside rippled in rhythm, and the man who walked beside her rested one hand on her back. It reminded Sam of having to hold his big sister's hand.

"Hoo-oo, Betsy, my girl," said Mr. Benson, and she halted. His voice was fond, full of respect. How strange, thought Sam, that these men relied on a partner who not only knew nothing at all about electricity but couldn't even talk.

When Sam delivered the water, Mum asked him, "Could you help unpack so there'll be room for the men to sit down? These saucepans can all hang on nails beside the stove. Here's the hammer."

"I can do the nails if you'll show me where you want them," Kate offered.

"You'll smash your thumb," predicted Sam, wanting to keep the hammering job for himself.

"Not if I wear an oven mitt."

The mitt took some mighty whacks, but a nail was eventually driven into the log wall, and Sam hung the spaghetti pot on it. Then Kate drove another underneath for the sieve. They got a great charge out of this. A house you could hammer nails into without worrying about chipping plaster or splitting wires was as much fun as a playhouse.

"What do we do with the empty box?" asked Sam.

"Make a pile of them up the hill and we'll burn them and roast marshmallows tonight," said Mum. So he flung the first empty out the back door.

Kate was still hammering away when a man came in to drill a hole for the phone wire.

"A hammer and a drill together is too much noise in this little place," said Mum. "Take a break, kids. Good news! I've found the bug repellent."

While Sam hovered near the man with the drill, Kate went outdoors with the bug lotion. She sat on the back doorstep to dab it over her arms, neck, and face, gingerly at first but with more confidence when she found it didn't hurt. Maybe her skin was really healed at last.

Her fingers explored the still unfamiliar surface, which felt like a marbled pebble worn partly smooth by water but still ridged and creased. She tried to compare it in her mind's eye with what she had seen there before, to make sense of it, so she could understand what people saw in her, what she was and what she was growing into, ever since that one minute last winter that had turned her life inside out.

2

Disaster

It had started with such a small thing. Kate was painting a poster about clean air for a competition. The day before the deadline, she set to work right after school. Mum had to take Sam out to buy shoes, so Kate was by herself in the house until Dad came home from work. The radio was on to scare away burglars, and she worked quickly to its rhythm, using the new paints Dad had given her for Christmas to fill in her sketch with bold strokes.

One half of the poster showed a factory belching smoke into brown clouds, while the other half showed children playing beside a green tree under a blue sky clear of everything but birds and sunshine. A white horse and a brown rabbit nibbled lush green grass and buttercups.

The oil paints were very co-operative about staying where she put them instead of running like the water-based colours she was used to. They could even be layered on top of one another without showing through. She made the horse's forelock lift airily over the background, then spangled the grass with daisies to use up her white paint. Soon the best poster she had ever done was drying on her easel in a corner of the kitchen. Richly satisfied, she began to tidy up. She rinsed the brushes carefully in plenty of turpentine and poured it down the kitchen sink.

There were a few sluggish glugs and the sink backed up.

She turned on the hot water to flush it through, but the water stayed put, mingling with the turpentine and paint in an ugly brew. She poked down the drain with a paintbrush, but nothing gave.

This was serious. Her mother would come home soon to cook dinner and Kate would be in big trouble. That might be the end of being allowed to do her artwork in the kitchen — or anywhere. If she didn't want to be hauled along on boring expeditions to boys' shoe departments, she would have to take decisive action.

Kate pulled a chair to the sink and climbed on it to root in the high cupboard where cleaning materials were kept. She found a big bottle of something that claimed to cut through grease like a laser beam. The liquid in the sink lay in greasy-looking swirls, so she poured in a good dose of grease-cutter. It gave off a sharp smell, but the turpentine didn't drain away.

Kate had another look in the cupboard. She found oven cleaner, weed killer, and insect repellent.

Because the top shelf was above her head, she had to crane her neck and lift the cans and bottles one by one to read the labels.

Any minute now, Mum would come back and demand, "What on earth have you done to the sink?" Kate's fingers fumbled quickly to the back of the shelf. And there — Eureka! an ancient can of drain opener. In haste she started opening it and stepped backwards off the chair.

At various times, Kate had been told or learned from experience not to do too many things at once, such as tying shoelaces while eating toast. If you hold the toast in your spare fingers, you get jam on your laces and dust on your toast, and if you clamp the whole slice between your teeth it breaks off and lands on your shoes, jam side down of course. But there are plenty of things that *can* be done efficiently at the same time, such as brushing your teeth while you read. Kate had always maintained that you couldn't know until you tried whether something was a great timesaver. If she had felt less hurried, though, she might have reflected that opening a can with your arms stretched above your head while stepping backwards off a chair is probably not a smart way to save time. Especially if the can contains poison.

The chair wobbled, she waved her arms to steady herself, and the drain opener splashed right onto her face. Screaming with pain, she dropped the can, and it rolled into the sink with a splash as she fell forward onto the counter. She felt for the tap, turned it on, and tried to splash water onto her eyes. But the sink was so full that she ended up splashing on a handful of the turpentine mixture, which hurt worse than ever. And clouds of choking gas were boiling out of the sink. She slipped down onto the floor.

She cried out for help, but the gas stung her throat and took the strength out of her voice. Anyway, there was no one to hear.

She had a dim notion that the gas was unhealthy and she ought to get away from it, but the pain of her face blotted everything else out. She had never realized it was possible to hurt so much. Her eyes felt as if someone was piercing them with a flaming torch. She squeezed them tight and tried rubbing them with her hands, but the poison seared her knuckles.

She staggered to her feet, trying to grope her way upstairs to the bathroom to get her head under cold water. Her fingers touched something sticky. A second later, the easel crashed down and knocked her feet from under her. Lying on the floor in the ruins of her artwork, she decided it was all too horrible to be real. Maybe in a dream she had stumbled into the ugly half of her poster, and there was nothing to do but wait for somebody to pull her out into the sunny green half.

The radio went on and on about a boy who had got lost in a snowstorm in his backyard and was dying of hypothermia.

After a lot of bad dreaming, Dad came home and found her. He asked her questions but she couldn't find her voice to answer them. She wanted to say she was sorry but the words wouldn't come out. He stood over her and cursed, saying things she'd never heard him say before, so it felt even more unreal. Then he called an ambulance.

Soon Mum and Sam came home. Mum was all for driving Kate straight to the hospital, but Dad wanted to wait for the ambulance. They hunted, coughing, for the first-aid book, and wrapped Kate in a blanket, and then the ambulance roared up.

At the hospital they gave Kate a needle and everything slipped away into nothingness.

When she came to, she had a bandage over her face so she couldn't see anything. The pain had shrunk to a soreness with sharp points in it now and then. Chickadees were chirping somewhere, a promising sign that she was back in the right side of the picture.

She felt weak as a new-hatched chick and would have fallen asleep again, but someone was crying close by. It sounded like a girl almost as old as herself, only she was crying steadily like a baby. Kate asked, "What's the matter?" There was no answer, only the same honking cry out of both nose and throat, a horrible noise going on and on until you wanted to do anything to stop it. "I wish you'd be quiet," Kate muttered, again without result. Perhaps the person was in another room. Perhaps they were deaf. Perhaps they were so miserable they didn't care. Kate tossed restlessly. Nobody had a right to keep other people awake that way. She felt like throwing a pillow at the whiner. But there was nothing she could do except try to think about something else.

She had come to this hospital once before, years ago. She had needed stitches in her leg, after falling off her bike when it was new and too big for her. Since then, of course, she had mastered that shining silver ten-speed that sheared into the wind, swift and silent as a gull. Soon the snow would be gone and she'd be skimming down the hill in the park, the wind whipping her hair, the green grass rolling beneath her, and trees in white and pink blossom arching over her.

It was a family ritual to strap the picnic basket to Dad's bike on the first fine Sunday in spring and pedal to the arboretum for a picnic by the lake. There was a tree whose blossoms trailed right to the ground, making a canopy just big enough for the four of them. She remembered draping herself along a branch and looking down on her parents, who smiled up at her, arm in arm. Wrapping her memories close around her, she drifted to sleep.

A clatter and the smell of food wakened her. This seemed strange because it was still dark. It was a moment before Kate realized the darkness was because her eyes were covered. They were very sore now. She put her hands up and felt the thick layers of gauze taped to her head.

"Mustn't touch your bandages," said a woman's voice. "I'm putting your tray on your table." Something bumped Kate's left elbow.

"What is it?" asked Kate.

"A sandwich and a milkshake," said the nurse.

"Milkshakes for breakfast, that's funny," said Kate.

"This is supper," said her mother. She sounded shaky, almost as if she had been sick in hospital herself. "How are you feeling, sweetie?"

"Not too bad, I guess." Somebody walked away — Kate hoped it was the nurse. She felt for the table beside her and found a cold plastic cup. As she lifted it toward her lips, something jabbed her in the cheek. She put the cup down in a hurry. It struck the edge of the tray and twisted out of her hand. She grabbed at it but couldn't find it, though she could feel milkshake soaking through the sheets onto her chest.

"It's okay, I've got it. Let me mop that up," said Mum kindly. Kate felt her dabbing with a rustly paper napkin. "Here, I'll put the straw in your mouth."

Kate opened her mouth, and this time she was poked, much more gently, on the tongue. When she said she'd had enough, her mother took the shake away and handed her something else. Her teeth closed on a shake-soggy peanut butter sandwich with paper napkin stuck to it. By the second mouthful she decided she wasn't hungry.

"I can't wait till I get these bandages off," said Kate.

There was a choking sound from the general direction of her mother. Then her father's voice said, more remotely, "It isn't going to make any difference."

"That's what you think," said Kate, a bit annoyed at him for keeping quiet so she hadn't known he was there. Annoyed also at the frozen quality of his voice when he contradicted her. All right, she'd been silly about the clogged sink, but she'd suffered enough for it. The whole top half of her face was burning like a colossal poison ivy rash. Surely Dad could show a bit of sympathy, as Mum did. Kate went on, "If you'd ever had to do things blindfold, you'd know it makes a big difference being able to see what you're eating."

"You don't understand," said her father.

"Dennis!" warned her mother.

They both shut up then. But the alarm in Mum's voice told Kate something was terribly wrong. "You don't mean . . ." She tore at the bandages. The adhesive tape stuck to her cheeks as tight as the skin itself, which protested savagely. Her mother's hands closed over hers, forcing them away.

"You *mustn't*, Katie. There's a chance we'll be able to get your sight back with another operation, later on when you're stronger," said Mum.

"A fair chance, fifty-fifty, according to the doctors," Dad said in that frozen voice.

Kate couldn't believe her ears. This had to be a nightmare — if it was this dark she couldn't be awake. But her mother was pinning her hands down to the bed in a terribly real grip, her arms trembling.

"No!" cried Kate, in a great, sobbing shriek.

"Don't cry, Katie," said Mum urgently. "The bandages will fall apart, and you need them."

Kate gasped. The whole living world of colour and light was gone from her and they wouldn't even let her cry! Her eyes stung furiously, as if that horrible poison was eating into them afresh, but no tears came. They didn't feel like proper eyes at all, only hurting flesh. Her stomach heaved, and she doubled up and vomited all over her lap. Mum quickly let her hands go.

"Get her head over the wastepaper basket," said Dad.

"I can't touch anything, my hands are filthy," Mum protested. She stretched her arms awkwardly around Kate's shoulders. "Sweetie, I know you feel terrible, we all do, but it's not the end of the world. You've still got us."

"Come on, you're a big girl, you can handle it," said Dad. "Nurse! Over here!"

Kate went on retching. The sickly-sweet hospital meal poured out of her, bitter with stomach acid. This couldn't be real, they couldn't expect her to swallow it. She heaved for all she was worth, until her nose ran and her ears popped. At last, feeling like a wrung-out rag, she sank back. And went on shaking.

People bustled about stripping off the sheets, and hands wiped her face briskly with a towel. She knew she must look absolutely disgusting.

"Mum, are you there?"

"Your mother's gone to wash her hands. You got her pretty dirty," the nurse said.

There was a fierce stinging in Kate's lap. "I want a shower," she said.

"No showers yet, you aren't strong enough," said the nurse firmly.

They took off her nightgown and washed her

thoroughly. It was horrible. The worst was not knowing how many people were seeing her naked. Was her father still there, still stonily silent? Was she in a ward full of other patients and their parents? Not knowing who was looking at you was unbearable, and yet she couldn't do anything about it. If she howled like that other girl had done, people would get fed up with her mighty quickly.

Somehow she would just have to learn to put up with things as they were. And if it hurt, she mustn't react, because that only made things worse.

All the family were so upset they all said it must be somebody else's fault. The doctors said if her eyes had been flushed out right away with water, they might have been saved, so Mum said Dad should have carried Kate upstairs to the bathtub and held her face under the tap as soon as he found her. Dad countered that Mum should not have told her to clean up without telling her how; a girl of her age, he said, should be taught by her mother what cleansers don't mix. Mum flared up at the sexist assumption that cleaning house had to be women's work. Furthermore, she pointed out, these new paints had been supplied by clever old Dad. Why did he always give the children things to make a mess with but take no responsibility for the trouble that followed? She also blamed him for breaking the bad news to Kate so harshly. But Dad accused her of being unrealistic and keeping the children in a dream world.

Sam remarked that their parents had screwed up

again. Kate retorted that Sam couldn't talk, because he had worn holes in his sneakers and needed new ones after only three weeks.

Deep down, though, she knew that although her family were too sorry for her to say a word of reproach and relieved their feelings by blaming one another, the accident was all her own stupid fault. But there was no use trying to turn over a new leaf and cause no more trouble. When they let her out of hospital, she found that in simply trying to walk across the living room, she knocked over lamps and flowerpots and crucial chess games. Instead of the responsible young lady her parents had (sometimes) been proud of, she was a junior Attila the Hun. She couldn't even put back what she knocked over. And she was forever making them late, because she took twice as long to get dressed or eat a meal. And when they finally did get her out the door in a matched pair of boots, somebody (usually Mum) had to hold her hand and guide her, as if she were a small child again.

The world was suddenly full of unseen hazards, of crimes waiting to be committed. After Kate had tripped over a toddler or two in a shopping plaza and knocked them howling to the terrazzo, her parents thought twice before taking her shopping. Since there was nothing for her to see, there was little pleasure in going out anyway. So she stayed home, and somebody stayed with her. Usually it was Mum, although Mum complained that Dad was an extravagant shopper.

They talked about sending Kate to a special

school for the "visually challenged", which was the fashionable term for blind. But Kate did not feel up to starting a new school just yet. She was still weak from the gas. Also there was the chance, though not a very good chance, that if she had some fancy microsurgery in a few months when the tissues had healed and she was strong enough to stay under anaesthetic for several hours, she might regain part of the use of one eye, perhaps enough to read a word at a time under a powerful magnifying glass. So, apart from a tutor who came a couple of hours a week, they left her alone.

Before long, Kate discovered that the worst thing about losing your sight is the boredom. It was like being stuck in a waiting room with nothing to read and no window to look out. She would have given anything just to ride her bike around the block and look at the neighbours' little clumps of crocuses pushing through the slush. TV programs were maddening when you couldn't see what people were talking about. That left radio and being read to by Mum.

Even things you didn't really need sight to enjoy were not as much fun as before. When friends came over, there wasn't as much joking. Since she couldn't see their faces, it was hard to guess what they were thinking. They sounded pitying, embarrassed, and bored, and they didn't stay long. She had the awful feeling that she made everyone around her unhappy. Nothing much was said around the supper table but "Stop kicking your chair, Sam."

The thunderbolt really shouldn't have taken

them by surprise, she thought afterwards. One morning at breakfast, their mother let the cocoa boil over. That was nothing really out of the ordinary, but what was unusual was how loudly and angrily she swore back at the hissing mess. Kate, suspecting that the strain of looking after her was getting to her mother, felt guilty and said nothing. But Sam, who was less inhibited about speaking up on the rare occasions when he noticed such things, demanded, "Is something bugging you?"

"Your father," said Mum bitterly, "is leaving us. Moving out."

Neither Sam nor Kate said anything. Kate was afraid that if she spoke, their mother would start crying. She also thought she had been dumb not to see this coming. Their father had become more and more remote as the winter wore on. He would come home very late in the evenings and sit silent in front of the TV, so Kate often couldn't tell if he was there.

Sam gulped down his burnt cocoa and escaped to school. Envying him, Kate had to stay and listen to their mother call a lawyer.

That afternoon, as she sat in the lawyer's waiting room while Mum discussed custody and dividing up assets, Kate realized that the corrosive poison that had eaten into her face was still at work, destroying her whole family.

Kate had Mum read the separation agreement to her and explain it. But no matter how precise the lawyers tried to make it, what came out of it was confusion. More and more confusion, like a bad dream.

Once Dad's things were moved out to an apartment in centretown, a real estate agent brought in troops of strangers who talked callously about knocking down walls and ripping up floors. Mum spent anxious weeks stuffing all their clutter into drawers to make the house presentable. At last one of the floor-rippers rose to the lure, and the home where Kate and Sam had been born was no longer theirs.

Then all the clutter had to come out and be packed up for the cabin or sold at a giant yard sale. The floor was littered with piles that Kate kept stumbling into. While her mother frantically packed, Kate was as useless as a baby. She and Sam spent the last days camping in their father's apartment, which smelled like another waiting room with its factory-new carpeting. Cynthia, their father's new girlfriend, had her own apartment next door, but she wandered in and out, speaking to them with the shallow sweetness of a dentist's receptionist, which she was. Kate found it unnerving to be around someone whose face she couldn't picture. Sam said Cynthia looked like she was cut out of a glossy magazine, with a frozen smile. The clatter of her shoes made Kate afraid her toes would be crushed by a vicious three-inch spike.

Supper in Dad's apartment was pizza in front of the TV. During the commercials Kate and Sam spread out their sleeping bags in the living room and settled in for the night with a bag of potato chips. This used to be their idea of a good time, but after the third night even Sam got fed up with sleeping on chip crumbs. Though they used to grumble when their parents sent them to bed by eleven on weekends, it hurt that neither parent now cared enough or had the energy to nudge them into a healthy life. Kate and Sam would amble along until Mum remembered to ask how long it was since they had had a shower, and it would be five days. At Dad's they did keep clean because he had a swirling hot tub, but they ate no vegetables, and toothbrushes stayed in the bottom of their bags.

Only once did Kate dare to interfere in all these new arrangements. When Dad taped on his expensive new stereo the old records that he and Mum couldn't agree to divide, Kate asked if he could keep the records and let them take the tapes to the cabin, because it was easier for her to drop a cassette into the ghetto-blaster than to handle a record. Not only did they agree, but Dad in an unusual burst of helpfulness offered to tape half a dozen of her favourites. Electronics was his home turf, for he was a computer systems analyst. Sam took after him. Like Dad, he would cheerfully fiddle with gadgets for her. But neither her father nor her brother would be seen with her in a restaurant because she spilled her food, and they hated leading her to the ladies' washroom and waiting by the door while she groped for the soap in the towel dispenser.

Kate could see some patterns in the confusion now, but the whole thing still didn't make sense. What could make a family stop being a family?

They had been knit together by so many things they needed from each other and enjoyed giving each other. Had Dad run away with Cynthia simply because she was a classier female to be seen with in a restaurant? And had that driven Mum to run away with Kate and Sam to the wilderness where nobody could see them?

From where Kate sat on the back doorstep of the cabin, the woods stretched north forever, broken only by lakes. The Canadian Shield, worthless for mechanized farms or skyscrapers or chemical plants, was the perfect shield for people who wanted to be alone.

The breeze on Kate's cheek smelled of cedar and long grass, with no trace of the left side of her poster. At last she was finished with waiting rooms and out in the free air. It was too bad she wasn't equipped to get the most out of it. Still, four out of five senses was not bad.

There had been a time when she felt empty. But something that had been slowly gathering together in the darkness had surfaced in last night's dream, filling her with the strength and confidence of a young horse. She felt there was an adventure waiting here. She began to sing:

> "Come saddle my horses and call out my men,
> Unhook the west port and let us go free . . ."

A telephone rang in the cabin. A man shouted out the front door, "We're hooked up at last! Come get your coffee!"

Kate went in to hear what the men had to say. Mum asked if anyone knew where she could buy free-range eggs, and the old man with the horse said he would be glad to supply her.

"We've got pretty near everything — hens, ducks, cattle, horses. It's still a real family farm, like in my grandfather's time."

"Where is it?" asked Mum.

"Up towards Middleville. Yellow frame house with 'Herbert Benson' on the mailbox. The wife's always there, just stop by."

"I'll try to make it this afternoon, once we get things slightly under control here," said Mum. "There's such a lot that needs doing."

"Yes, you've got your work cut out if you're hoping to settle here," said Mr. Benson. "This used to be the Pippards' place, didn't it? Can't say I'm sorry they're gone."

"They aren't gone," contradicted the low-voiced man who had drilled the holes. "And I bet they still think they own it. If I were you, I'd put stronger locks on the doors."

"Did they live in the old farmhouse that burned down?" asked Sam.

The low-voiced man snorted. "They sure did. They were the ones who burned it."

Abruptly, the man who had said nothing so far stood up and said, "We'd better be going. Thanks for the coffee, Mrs. Linbert. I hope it works out for you here."

3

Enter the GG

At the Bensons' farmhouse, Mum told the children to stay in the car and went to knock at the side door. Kate asked Sam, "Can you see the horses?"

"They're at the far side of a big field with a bunch of cows."

A stout lady with greying hair and glasses came to the door. Mum explained her business, and Mrs. Benson took her into the house. Then all was quiet except for the clucking of hens.

Presently a door groaned open. Mum came out of the house, clutching a flat of eggs and followed by Mr. and Mrs. Benson. He asked Mum if they would like to see the animals, and before she could frame a polite "yes", Sam and Kate both said it for her.

Mr. Benson led them to an old cedar-rail fence and whistled. Immediately a great thunder of hooves on grassy ground made Kate's breath catch in her throat. Three horses cantered across the field toward them. One Sam recognized as the square-built brownish mare he had seen that morning, and another was dark and heavy like her. But the leader was all white, his long mane and tail pluming out like wisps of cloud as he ran. Right up to the fence he charged, and skidded to a halt at the last possible moment. Then he reached his nose over the rails and blew on Mr. Benson's face.

The farmer stroked the broad white cheeks and said, "You're a fine fellow, Tweed." He gave the horse a carrot from his pocket.

"Why do you call him Tweed?" asked Mum. "He's the least tweedy of the bunch." Both the horses now trotting up had dark coats flecked with grey that looked like tweed jackets.

Mr. Benson cleared his throat. "It's short for Tweedsmuir."

"Oh, because he's a GG?" asked Mum.

"What's a geegee?" asked Kate.

"A horse, fuzzhead," said Sam.

"It's short for governor general," Mum explained. "Lord Tweedsmuir was one of our governors general and also a terrific writer. He used to be called John Buchan."

"So did this horse," said Mrs. Benson. "When he was a little fellow he used to put on tremendous bucking displays just for fun, so we called him Johnny Buckin'. My son got dumped off regular when he was breaking the colt. Later, Johnny settled down and became respectable, and Father wanted another name for him because the neighbours had a dog called Johnny. So we promoted him to the title old King George gave John Buchan: Lord Tweedsmuir."

Mr. Benson shot his wife the very look Mum had given Sam when he told someone who was thinking of buying their house that the basement turned into a lake in early spring. Sam guessed Mr. Benson didn't want them to know the horse had bucked people off, probably because he hoped to sell him. But Mum, not catching that look, laughed and said, "That's perfect," and patted the horse. She laid Kate's hand on his cheek.

Kate was delighted. A bookish pun was the one thing that would make her mother take kindly to a large, expensive animal that needed a lot of looking after. "He seems very friendly," she said.

"He's a pet," agreed Mrs. Benson. "He followed Keith around like a dog. When Keith phones from Calgary, he always asks after Tweed. He was upset when we told him about this nasty cut on his neck. Father was upset, too, when he got the vet's bill. Can you imagine, two hundred dollars just to stitch it up? So Father said, that's it, we can't keep the horse if Keith isn't coming back. And Keith agreed we should sell him as soon as the wound looks okay."

Kate's breath came shorter. She was glad Mrs. Benson had let her mother know he was for sale, but a hefty vet bill would scare her off. Mrs. Benson's motorized tongue was a real hazard.

Meanwhile, Tweed looked his visitors over with an intelligent eye. He turned to Sam and blew gently on his face.

Sam was used to dismissing horses as girls' stuff — cutesy little plastic ponies with long nylon hair, spangled unicorns with dumb names like Moonbeam. But this animal had nothing at all cute about him. He had burrs in his hair and mud on his legs. The L-shaped cut on his neck looked like a hockey skate injury, swollen and stiff with dried blood. Yet he was handsome in his way — you couldn't help liking those big sweeps of muscle. He looked fit to partner a hard-working phone crew and ready to race for fun, to show off his strength. "How did he cut himself?" Sam asked.

"Leaning over a strand of barbed wire to eat the grass in the next field," said Mr. Benson. "He thinks it's greener."

Sam grinned. Any right-minded animal must get tired of being penned up in the same field all the time. "Do they live here all year round?" he asked.

"Yes. They like being outdoors, even in winter."

"So they aren't hard or expensive to look after?" asked Kate eagerly.

"Oh no," said Mr. Benson, who seemed quite ready to spin the sales pitch with Kate. "Just grass in summer and hay in winter. They don't need grain unless they're working hard. Tweed hasn't tasted oats in so long he wouldn't recognize them, but he's as sound as a bell, aren't you, my lad?" Kate heard the bellish sound of a slap on the horse's neck, or maybe flanks. "Look at those straight legs. His sire was a Thoroughbred, a racehorse."

"Very pretty," said Mum vaguely. "Well, thanks so much for letting us see them, and for the eggs.

We mustn't leave them sitting in the hot car. Come along, kids." She sounded anxious to get away, as if she had finally twigged to a plot to make her buy something that cost more than a dollar-eighty a dozen.

In the car, Kate asked, "What did the horses look like?"

"Tweed was the best," answered Sam. "He looks white coming towards you, but his back is mixed grey and white, and his rear end is dark so the tail stands out white against it."

"Sounds like a dapple grey," said Kate. The colour of her dream horse. Taking a deep breath, she said, "You know, we have room for a horse now."

Mum blew out sharply. "Don't start getting ideas. A large animal is a big responsibility. It's for people who know what they're doing."

"But this horse is used to getting hardly any attention. His only problem is with barbed wire, and our fence doesn't have any of that, does it?"

"No, Katie, but there could be all kinds of other accidents we wouldn't know how to prevent. Anyway, if you keep a horse you need to groom it and exercise it and you need to know when it's sick. None of us knows how to do that, and I don't have time to learn. As soon as we get electricity in the cabin, I have to knuckle down to serious translating. I've hardly earned a cent in three months, and moving has been very expensive."

"But I have time," said Kate, "and I learned a lot at riding camp last summer."

"In four weeks you can't have learned enough to

take responsibility for a horse, especially when you can't see it. I'm sorry, but there it is." Mum jammed her foot down on the brakes, making them all lurch. Then Kate felt the car turn a corner and pick up speed, purring on the paved highway. She kept her mouth shut. It was true she couldn't look after the horse on her own, and it would be unfair to demand help from her mother, who already had to do so many extra things for her. Yet what she felt like saying was, "I've always wanted a horse, and there's so much now that I want and can't have, please won't you give me this one thing to make up for not seeing flowers and faces and living in my own house with my own two parents?" But saying that would just make it all worse.

In the tense silence, Sam looked at his mother, hunched frowning over the wheel, and at Kate, whose mouth was puckered up on the verge of tears. Those irritating females had forgotten all about him. They almost deserved to be as miserable as they were making themselves. Didn't they care what he wanted? Didn't they realize how competent he was? "I wouldn't mind having a horse," he said. "That Tweed is a boy's horse, anyway. Though maybe I'd rather have a dog."

"Oh come *on*, you guys," said Mum. "The cabin is barely big enough for the three of us. If we have to get a guide dog for Kate later on, that will be more than enough. Let's not talk about animals till we've got our lives sorted out."

Up the hill behind the house was a fire pit lined

with stones. Here they made a bonfire of their moving boxes, and roasted the Bensons' eggs between the heated stones. At first Kate found it scary to sit near an open fire she couldn't see. When the flames suddenly roared loud, she was afraid they were jumping out at her. She sat so far back that her marshmallows took forever. Mum gave her a couple of lightly toasted ones to keep her going, but it was frustrating. She used to be the family artist with an untwisted coat-hanger, giving her marshmallows a crisp, dark-brown, blistered crust and a melting inside, just a second short of burning. She asked Sam to tell her when hers got to that stage, but it browned so slowly that he forgot it until it burned. He liked his to blaze up, anyway.

Mum read out loud a book about the pioneers. At first when she had begun reading to Kate, Sam had disliked it because it made them seem like little kids again. But it was not a bad way to fill the silence while he singed one last marshmallow and watched the sunset die down behind the woods and the first stars come slowly alight. A whippoorwill sang close by, and other hidden creatures made little noises, but only the brook across the road still had the energy to sing the song it had chanted all day.

Next morning the electrician, Mr. Hunt, was due to start work. He turned up at noon, looking as if he had just been hauled out of bed. Mum did her best to make the work sound simple — "just wiring for a couple of lights, the fridge and the computer, and of course the pump." They needed an electric pump to supply running water from their well, which was across the field where the old farmhouse had stood.

Mr. Hunt said the pump would need a separate hook-up to the hydro pole, and a whole building would have to be put up to protect the pump and the well. He thought it would probably be cheaper to drill a new well up by the cabin and build a little shelter against the wall. But that was a gamble, he allowed, for the cost of the well depended on how far down you had to drill before you found clean water.

Kate and Sam heard their mother's voice rising anxiously, for she hated gambling. When Mr. Hunt dropped his cigarette butt on the wooden floor and ground it with his heel, Sam was afraid she would start yelling. But she only said, "Please make a start on wiring the house, and I'll figure out about the well later."

While Mr. Hunt went to his car for tools, Sam asked her, "Are we going to get a new well?"

"I don't know. The other one is perfectly good and thirty metres deep. Maybe we could get a hand pump for it."

"But it would be no fun carrying all our water in pails from way over there. It's like halfway round the block."

She searched his eyes, looking through him for an answer. Sam blinked. He could still hardly realize he was the only one left in the family she could look in the eye. Finally she said, "I guess you're right, though I'm afraid we're looking at another two thousand dollars we don't have. I'll call the driller."

Sam was pleased. When the driller said he'd be

there next afternoon, Sam generously took the buckets to the creek for a refill without even being asked.

The next phone call was another matter. Mum answered it. She didn't a moment later say "Speaking" or "Oh hello, how are you?" She just sat listening while the other person talked, and her shoulders tensed up. At last she said, "They can't come here, the place is a construction site. You'll have to put them off." After a pause, she said, "Well, why couldn't you have arranged something for the weekend?" Hearing her angry tone, Sam and Kate knew their father must be on the line.

After more arguing, they heard Mum arrange to take them into Ottawa the next morning and drop them off at a hotel. Sam was indignant that plans had been made for him without anyone asking what he wanted. Kate also cringed at the thought of being dumped in an unfamiliar place with a lot of strange people.

After Mum hung up, she said, "Mr. and Mrs. Linbert are coming to town and want to see you. I'll take you in tomorrow morning, and Dennis will bring you home in the evening." She sounded as if she was talking about strangers, not Grammy and Grandpa and Dad.

It was as if their parents had been held together by an elastic band, Kate thought. Sometimes they used to pull a little apart and make it twang, but it had always snapped back — always, until the day it was stretched too far and broke, and the ends stung them in the face. Kate had comfortably believed her parents were united by a solid gold wedding band, but all that was left now was like a limp strand of broken rubber.

What made it worse was thinking the weight that had stretched the band beyond its limit was the burden of their blind daughter.

"But I want to watch them dig the well," Sam objected. "Machinery that cuts through hundreds of metres of bedrock must be really something."

"No," said Mum. "And speaking of water, you need baths. Tonight you'll wash yourselves from head to foot in the dishpan."

"The dishpan! Yeeuck!" protested Sam loudly. "Why can't we go swimming?"

"Lower your voice, it's going straight through my head. And please be reasonable. I have a lot of things to do, and now your father is making me drive an extra couple of hundred kilometres tomorrow."

"What's the good of living up here if you can't go swimming?" Sam demanded, and kicked the wall for emphasis. The logs didn't shudder like the Gyproc in their old house, and neither did his mother shout "Sa-am, you young delinquent!" as she used to. All the reaction he got was a deep bass thud and a martyred sigh.

"Couldn't Sam and I go for a dip in Waddle Creek?" Kate suggested. "It's not so deep you need a sighted buddy, is it?"

"There's a strong current and slippery stones. It would be hard going for you, and you couldn't do much to help Sam if he got into trouble." Mum sighed again. "I suppose we could drive over to Robertson Lake. They say there's a decent beach there."

After nineteen kilometres of gravel road that wound and plunged like a rollercoaster, Mum grumbled, "This had better be an awfully good lake. If we meet another car on these bends, we're done for." But the twentieth kilometre ended in a pot of liquid gold, a clear blue lake that stretched into vistas of wooded islands. A handful of cottages perched on the shore, and far out on the water someone was fishing from a canoe, but not a soul was swimming.

They parked on grass under silver birches and crossed the soft white sand to the water's edge. Sam forged ahead and launched joyfully into a splashy crawl. But Kate, holding tight to her mother's hand, took three cautious steps into the water and said, "Wait a minute, Mum."

This was the first time she had tried to swim since losing her sight, and she felt more fear than she'd known since she first learned to stay afloat. Suppose when she thought she was making for shore she actually headed out into the cold deeps where no one could help her? There was also an undercurrent of formless fear, of slimy horrors that pulled you down and choked you.

"Come on, there aren't any hidden rocks. Don't be a wuss," called Sam.

That was too much. Freeing her hand from her mother's, Kate propelled herself into a front glide.

Moments later, her worries were forgotten in the bliss of twisting and darting through the cool and friendly water. She enjoyed it more than ever before, because once she had satisfied herself there were no rocks or sea monsters, she could revel in the rare joy of moving freely without crashing into anything. Also, when she dived, she was for once as invisible to other people as they were to her.

"How come we have to get so clean for Grammy and Grandpa?" asked Sam, on principle.

"You know how fussy they are," said Mum. "And they don't approve of us living at the cabin."

"What do they think we should be doing instead?" asked Kate.

"They want you to go to a residential school for the blind near where they live. I don't know what they have in mind for Sam, but I bet it's something with flush toilets and all that jazz. So for goodness sakes, when you're with them, keep quiet about the biffy and no fridge, or they'll sick the health inspector on us. Try to make a good impression."

"Could they really make us move?" asked Sam.

"They could make it horribly unpleasant for us all. Your father usually goes along with them, too, and he can do quite a lot of damage when he tries. We could end up in court, fighting for custody. Then whoever could afford the best lawyers would win — and it wouldn't be me."

"I didn't think he wanted us," said Sam.

"Not to live with him in the apartment," said Mum. "But he wouldn't mind sending you to boarding school if his parents paid the bill."

Kate shivered. There had been more than enough fighting already. And the last thing she wanted was to live in a strange school. Grammy and Grandpa, though, were strong-minded people, accustomed to making things happen their way.

4

Impressionists

The hotel their grandparents had selected as an adequate place to spend the night was as unlike Kate and Sam's cabin as a place could be. In the past, Grammy and Grandpa had always slept in the guest room at their house when they came for a visit. Now that Dad was living in an apartment with no guest room, his parents stayed in a hotel, like grand, forbidding strangers. Kate felt the marble floor and icy air-conditioning, and Sam's eye was caught by polished brass ashtrays. After their mother phoned up to the grandparents' room, they waited on an overstuffed silk couch that seemed designed to tip them onto the floor.

Grammy's voice as she stepped off the elevator was full of forced sweetness. She kissed both children. Sam, who was not big on public kisses, cringed as he pecked at her powdered cheek. Kate did her dutiful best to return Grammy's embrace, but since she hadn't become expert at kissing people she couldn't see, her lips landed on Grammy's sharp metal earring and dug it into her neck.

Mum said she had to be hurrying back to see the well-driller. Grammy said, "Are you sure you won't stay for a cup of tea, Irene?" — but not as if she would really enjoy visiting with her.

"Where's Grandpa?" asked Sam, when their mother had left them standing in the middle of the lobby.

"He had to go to a meeting, dear. We'll be having lunch with him later on. What would you like to do in the meantime? Shall we have a cup of something in the coffee shop?"

"No, thank you," said Kate. Two strange restaurants in a day were more than she could handle.

"Is there anything you need that I could buy you? Clothes or shoes?"

"No, thank you," said both children. Grammy looked them over narrowly from head to toe. Though they had put on their cleanest clothes and Kate was actually wearing a dress and a shoulder bag, Sam saw in her face that they didn't measure up to her standard of perfect-looking grandchildren. He had an awful fear she was itching to buy him another bow tie. To fend her off, he added, "We don't have room for any more things at the cabin, it's too small."

"I see," said Grammy, with a long face, and Kate thought maybe that had not been such a smart answer. "Then would you like to go to a museum? There are two or three close by, and the gallery. They tell me the Impressionists are well worth seeing."

Kate held back from asking, Are they worth standing in front of if you can't see them? Sam asked, "What are Impressionists?" He had an idea they were like illusionists, which was Grammy's word for magicians.

"French painters from a hundred years ago. They're very famous and their work is beautiful. I think you ought to see them, and . . . but Katherine, I suppose it would be boring for you, dear," she ended lamely. "I wish there was a concert I could take you to, but there's no matinee today."

Sam silently thanked the musicians' union for that.

"We could go to the Museum of Natural Science if you'd prefer," Grammy offered. "It has films, you could listen to the sound-track."

"No, thanks. There are too many little kids running around."

"Katherine, you used to be so fond of smaller children. You mustn't let yourself get bitter," Grammy reproached.

"Sorry," mumbled Kate.

"She bumps into them," Sam explained. "Then their mothers yell at her, and Mum does a big apologizing routine."

"I see," said Grammy with another long face. There was a strained silence. They seemed to have been standing in the lobby for a very long time.

Kate remembered how keen her grandmother always was to go to art exhibits and concerts, living as she did in a small, dull, and distant town. Kate was bound to be bored no matter what they did. There was no sense in all three of them being bored, and after all, Grammy was the visitor. She said, "I'll go to the gallery with you if you like. There are hardly any little kids, and the paintings are hung high on the walls where they can't trip you, like the things in the museum."

It wasn't easy, though. Grammy was not used to leading anyone, and she made a nervous and confusing guide. She said, "Look out for the mailbox!" when it was a block away, yet she stepped off the curb without warning, making Kate stumble. The sign at the gallery said, "Please use revolving doors," and Grammy, being a person who always obeyed instructions, bundled Kate into a compartment, stepped into the one behind her, and shoved. Kate was knocked off balance and banged her head on the partition behind her, sending her sunglasses flying.

Grammy was so busy clucking, "Oh dear, I'm so sorry, did you hurt yourself? Don't step on your glasses," that she forgot to tell Kate to get out until it was too late. Standing inside the gallery, Grammy tried to move the door backwards to free Kate, but it would go only one way. So Kate had to keep on revolving. When she reached the outside again, Sam stepped in beside her, laughing.

"Care for another spin?" he asked.

"Drop dead," said Kate fiercely.

Obligingly, Sam keeled over, barely recovering in time to get them both out of the door and hand Kate over to the arm of their agitated grandmother. Then he went back for another spin to pick up her glasses.

A security guard advanced toward them with a dagger face that made Sam crack up and brought a blush to Grammy's powdered cheeks. She said faintly, "We'd like to see the Expressionist Inhibition . . . I mean, the Impressionist Expo . . . uh, do you have a guidebook?"

Sam didn't find the show as boring as he'd thought he might. The security arrangements were interesting: electronic beams were pointed at certain pictures, ready to scream if anyone touched them. When Grammy discovered that, she parked Kate on a chair in the middle of the room so she wouldn't accidentally set the alarms off and bring the security guards down on their heads again. As for the pictures, they were pleasant enough, though there were a ridiculous lot of females, either decked out in frills and ruffles like old lampshades or showing mounds of marbled pink and purple flesh like raspberry ripple ice cream. There was hardly a boy anywhere on the yards of canvas, except for a group of jockeys. Sam liked that picture, because you could almost feel the wind blowing the clouds and whipping the horses' tails as they keyed up for the start of their race.

At least there are no blackflies, Kate thought to herself, and it's not too hot. Also no breeze, no birdsong, no quiet and no single thing to do. Another dentist's waiting room, in fact. But maybe it would put Grammy into a good mood so she wouldn't try to drive them away from their cabin and nag Dad to take custody of them. Because, although she still had some feeling for Dad, it would be unbearable to have him take them just because his mother made him. He would have to show he really wanted them. And even then, how could they trust him?

One arm of her dark glasses had cracked in the revolving door, so they kept slipping down her face.

As she sat there doing nothing, the busyness of last summer at the riding camp came back to her: bustling around a barn with currycombs and dandybrushes, trotting across the fields of waving Queen Anne's lace with kids her own age. She longed to see the graceful arc of a horse rising over a jump. Even more, she ached for the warm feel of a silky coat, the swift and sure movement of hooves under her. If only . . .

In the empty air of the hushed gallery, she began to build a dream castle.

Grandpa met them for lunch in a downtown restaurant with heavy cloth napkins. They were invited to order whatever they liked. This gave Kate an uncomfortable feeling that they were expected to pay for their meal in information, like secret agents. Sure enough, as soon as the waiter had taken their orders, Grandpa said, "Now, tell us about this cabin on Waddle Creek Road." His tone was lightly ironic, as if the idea of living there was as ridiculous as the name.

"It's just a cabin," shrugged Sam. "Big logs fitted together at the corners."

Kate knew they wanted more. "It's halfway up a hill. You go up three steps to the front door, but the back door is nearly level with the ground. There's a loft half the length of the cabin, and stairs running up to it. Sam and I share the loft, with curtains between our rooms."

If the grandparents were impressed by how well Kate could describe a place she'd never seen, they didn't say so. Grammy merely asked, "Where does your mother sleep?"

"In a hammock below us," said Kate. "She rolls it up and stows it in a corner in the morning."

"Like a sailor," chuckled Grandpa.

"Yes," agreed Kate, "it's quite a bit like living in an old sailing ship, because everything is made of wood, and every inch of indoor space counts, though there's all kinds of room outdoors. We've been singing sea shanties." That morning, in fact, they had gone right through "Barrett's Privateers." Mum never let them sing that when anyone was in earshot, because the way they belted out "God damn them all!" blew people's socks off. But at the cabin there was no one to hear even the full force of Sam's formidable lungs except rabbits and chipmunks. That was one of the best things about the cabin. But you couldn't tell that to Grammy.

"Are you happy there?" asked Grammy earnestly.

"Yes," said Kate. She searched for an explanation her grandparents could understand. "It's *real*. The logs used to be real trees growing in the woods."

"You can imagine building it yourself, with an axe and a few pounds of nails," said Sam. He gestured at the papered walls and swirled stucco ceiling, things he'd never dream of fussing around with.

"But is it clean?" Grammy asked anxiously.

"Clean enough," said Sam. Kate said nothing because she didn't know, and this would not make her grandmother's mind easier.

"Are there things you don't like about it?" Grandpa asked casually, glancing up from the roll he was buttering.

"The blackflies," said Sam and Kate together.

"But they'll be over in a couple of weeks," Kate added, and kept quiet about the mosquitoes.

The waiter appeared, with steak and French fries for Sam and quiche for Kate because it didn't need serious cutting. The grandparents' salad plates seemed more in keeping with the weather, but after a couple of days in a fridgeless house where you had to light a fire before you could cook, Sam and Kate could see they were in for a long summer of carrots and peanut butter sandwiches. Only in the early mornings was the extra heat of the stove bearable.

Normally Mum told Kate what was on her plate

using a clock-face system: fried egg at four o'clock, homefries at eight, toast at twelve. Kate would have liked to know what was waiting to be spilled onto the stiff tablecloth, but she didn't want to draw attention to herself by asking. She ventured a couple of knife strokes, trying to tell by the resistance what was where. It was like a game of battleship, sending out random torpedoes to try to locate the unseen hazards before her.

Meanwhile, the cross-examination continued. "What do you do out there all day? Ride your bike, I suppose, Sam?" asked Grandpa.

"I hope you wear your helmet," said Grammy.

"It isn't like the city, Grammy. There's no traffic, and the roads are dirt. It's great," said Sam.

"Plenty of coasting on those hills, eh?" said Grandpa.

To coast down a hill on a bicycle, the wind lifting your hair and whistling in your ears, as the road rushes by underneath you . . . Kate gripped her knife and fork as if they were handlebars.

"Need help cutting up your dinner, Katherine?" asked Grammy.

"It's all right, thanks." She took a stab at her plate and put her fork in her mouth. There was nothing on it. She tried again, and speared a snowpea, which dropped off the fork when it touched her lips. On the third try, she nailed something heavy. Opening her mouth wide around it, she discovered it was almost the whole wedge of quiche. She crammed it firmly into her mouth. It was so big she couldn't move her jaws to chew it and had to wait for the crust to dissolve slowly down her throat. Her jaws ached from stretching. Everybody had stopped talking, and she felt them staring at her as if she were a chipmunk that had strayed in from the backwoods.

"Let me just cut up your potatoes for you, dear." Kate felt Grammy's slippery silk sleeve and bony wrist reach across her arm. Her mouth was too full to protest. "There now, try that."

Not since Kate was a baby had anybody interfered with her food like that. Had Grammy used her own knife and fork, and were there germs on them? Even if there weren't, it was outrageous for someone to mess up the food on her plate without asking her, and in public, too. "I wish . . ." she began, and then stopped, because you did after all have to be polite to the people who bought you your dinner.

"Yes, dear?" Grammy prompted helpfully.

Kate swallowed the last lump of quiche, groping for inspiration. "I wish someone would invent a bicycle with eyes."

They all laughed. It wasn't an altogether natural laugh — she rarely got a truly relaxed laugh from people these days. But it was better than the injured reaction she would get if she blurted out what she had started to say: I wish you'd keep your scrawny old hands off my food and not watch me.

"A bicycle with eyes . . . well, I haven't heard of that yet," said Grandpa. "But you know, there are some marvellous gadgets now. Computers with voice synthesizers that read back what you've typed. With that you could do the same work your mother does. You could also be a programmer or a receptionist, or a number of other things, besides a piano tuner, of course. Have you given any thought to what you'd like to be when you grow up?"

"Not really," said Kate. One day at a time was plenty to cope with. Actually, she thought of being a family court judge who put children's interests first in deciding custody cases, but she wasn't prepared to talk about that now. Anyway, surely she'd be able to see again by the time she grew up. She was thankful that at least Grammy and Grandpa were more refined than Uncle Jim, who always used to tease her about her boyfriends. He had given that up since the accident. Much as she had disliked being teased, the unspoken assumption that no boy would ever take an interest in her now was more maddening.

"You can be my assistant when I'm an inventor," said Sam generously. "I'll design the world's first seeing bike, and you can test-drive it for me. It will stop automatically when it comes to a red light, and tell you when the coast is clear."

"Instead of a combination lock, it should open when you say 'sesame snaps'," said Kate, warmed by his enthusiasm. "When you park it at a crowded bike rack, it will beep so you can find it."

"It doesn't sound cheap to manufacture," Grandpa said with a laugh.

"No, but don't worry, we'll give you a complimentary model," Sam smiled back.

"In the meantime, have you considered a tandem bike?" asked Grandpa.

Kate told him. "Mum wanted to get one she and I could ride together. The cheapest costs as much as a fifth of the cabin — that is, with all the land down to the road and along to the lilac tree and the barn."

Put like that, compared to solid logs and land that was forever, it was a ridiculous price for a piece of metal. It even blew some of Grandpa's executive cool. After a moment of silence, he said, "I'm afraid that's out of our league."

"Though we'd like to get you something that would give you pleasure up there," said Grammy. "Not that I can believe your mother really means to keep you in that primitive hut. She must realize you need to go to school —"

"But the school bus comes partway up the road already," said Sam.

"Yes, but a country school doesn't offer the kind of education you need to prepare you for real life. And besides, it isn't *safe* to stay in such a remote place, with no neighbours. Dennis tells me someone burned down the house that was there before, and the fire department knew nothing about it till it was all over. In an emergency you'd be helpless, a woman and two children."

"That happened years ago, and they caught the person who set the fire and put him in prison," said Sam. "It was someone who used to live in the house and got mad at his brother who was still living there. One of the guys who put in our phone started to tell me, though he wouldn't give me the whole story, for some reason."

"Don't worry about us, Grammy. We've got the phone," said Kate hastily. She was afraid she didn't sound very convincing, even to herself. Having caused one terrible accident, she would be thought unsafe until she somehow proved she could look after herself. But how could she do that as long as people insisted on standing over her and doing things for her?

Grandpa laid down his coffee cup and stood up. "I'm afraid I have to get back to work. See you later this afternoon." He laid his hand briefly on Sam's shoulder and dropped a quick kiss on Kate's cheek, giving her no time to return it.

Grammy was less inclined to argue when Grandpa wasn't there to back her up, or maybe keep her from going too far. She said brightly, "Now, what would you children like to do this afternoon? We have three hours until your father meets us."

Three hours of behaving nicely in a museum stretched before them like a low, grey rain cloud. Sam looked at his grandmother and saw a woman whom no power on earth would inveigle into a video arcade.

Kate cleared her throat. It was now or never. "Would it be really inconvenient to go to our bank?"

It was not really convenient, but they went anyway, because Kate made it plain that it was the one place she did want to go, and she wanted it more than the others wanted to go anywhere else they could agree on. They took a bus, which was a strain on Kate because she couldn't see what to hold on to and was afraid of sitting down on some stranger's lap. Sam, however, stood happily on the swirling table in the accordion-pleated middle of the bus.

When they reached the bank, Grammy asked, "Now, what is it you'd like me to do for you here?"

"It's all right, Sam can help me."

"What are you trying to do, anyway?" he asked her.

"Invest in our marvellous seeing-eye bike, of course," she whispered. "We need a pink slip that says 'Withdrawal'. Here's my pass book. How much is there in my account?"

"Six hundred and forty-two dollars and eighty-seven cents. Wow, I didn't know you were that rich."

"Remember I sold my bike and all that stuff at the yard sale. I want to withdraw six hundred and forty. Write that down, with the date and account number."

"But I haven't invented the bike yet."

"I'll explain later. Put your finger underneath where it says 'Signature' and I'll write my name."

The wad of twenties wouldn't fit into Kate's small purse, so Sam took a handful in his shorts pocket. "That looks like a lot of money for a young person to be carrying," said Grammy. "Are you sure you wouldn't like me to keep it safe in my purse?"

"It's all right, thanks," said Kate. In a day with Grammy, she seemed to be wearing those words out. "Now where shall we go?"

It was Sam's turn to pick. They ended up at the local park where they had spent many summer days since they were tiny. Soon Sam's friends, released from school, came drifting into the playground and they began punishing a soccer ball.

Grammy offered to push Kate on the swings. Imagining how silly she would look being pushed at her age by an elderly woman, Kate refused at first. But after they had sat a while on the bench listening to the soccer players yelling, she said, "Lead me to the swings and warn me if anyone gets in the way, please." Grammy seemed happy to help, though she stopped twice to shake sand out of her shoes. Kate gave her the sunglasses, since she was afraid they would fall off when she swung.

The swing soared like a bird, like a plane, like a bike coasting gloriously uphill. Kate pumped it so high it stalled at the top. Though she couldn't see the houses rising over the bar or the blur of the ground rushing up to meet her and then being left behind, the motion in itself was delight. It had been so long since she'd been able to run freely that she couldn't get enough of this hurtling through the air under her own steam.

"Hi, Kate," said a girl's voice below her, rather shyly.

"Hi," responded Kate, wondering who it was. She stopped pumping to listen. She became painfully conscious of the missing sunglasses. Nobody would tell her honestly what her face looked like, they kept assuring her it was fine really, nothing anybody would notice, but the skin felt so grainy that she was sure it was a hideous mottled purple and red.

Since the girl said nothing more, Kate asked, "Amy, is that you?" Amy lived just down the street and was often in the park.

"No, it's Jennifer." Kate ought to have known the voice after being in the same class for five years. "I thought you'd moved away," said Jennifer.

"We did, we're just in town for the day. How are things?"

"Okay, I guess. I'd better be going. See you around." Footsteps walked away over the asphalt.

"See you," said Kate shyly. Now that Jennifer was gone, there were fifty things she wanted to ask her about — friends and teachers and schoolyard feuds. She had a sudden, fierce wish to see a face again and share a smile, or even a grimace. This never seeing anybody's face was a real drag.

Kate stopped the swing. She wished she was back at the cabin. If you had to be lonely, it hurt less to be in your own private hideaway, where people didn't look at you and feel uncomfortable and run away. If only she had a friend who wouldn't run away and didn't care what she looked like. Who needed her. Who wanted to go places with her.

5

A Seeing Bike

Dad turned up late at the hotel, apologizing smoothly. He too had dressed to impress the grandparents and polished his manners. He could look quite elegant when he tried, for he was a tall man with classic features. Mum's friends said he was too good looking to be reliable, as well as too brainy. He went through life believing that when he had put in a correct appearance and favoured people with an intellectual analysis of a situation, it was quite unreasonable for anyone to expect more of him.

Back at his apartment he served them takeout ravioli, one of the few things Kate could eat in public without embarrassing him or needing help. The grandparents gave him the same kind of cross-examination the children had had at lunch, Grammy again sounding concerned and Grandpa sounding deliberately casual. They fished for information about Cynthia, but Dad steered the conversation toward his work and his apartment.

Sam drifted over to the TV, but his father said to him, "Pick us a record." Grammy disapproved of children watching too much TV. So Sam put on a Switched-On Bach.

"Your bike," Sam said to Kate, who was mending her sunglasses with electric tape, "could work like an electronic eye in a supermarket door. If it senses a large object like a car in front, it'll put on the brakes. The challenge will be making it go past parked cars. I guess you'll just have to listen, and if you don't hear an engine running, deactivate the brakes."

"No bicycle is going to detect a car approaching from the side without radar," said Kate. "You'll make it too heavy to pedal."

"I thought you were backing this invention," said Sam.

"The vehicle I have in mind doesn't need more inventing, Samuel. It can tell an idling car from a tree, it can handle all kinds of terrain, changes gears on its own and doesn't rust if you leave it out in the rain. And it will carry you and me both."

"You think you can get all that for six hundred and forty bucks?" scoffed her brother.

"I'm going to call and ask, anyway. *They*'re all busy." She jerked her head at the talkers around the table. "Come into the bedroom and dial for me, please."

"It's seven o'clock, all the stores will be shut."

"This isn't a store, it's a farm."

Light dawned on Sam. "Oh . . . you mean Tweed?"

"Of course. Come on." With her arms stretched in front of her, she led the way along the hall to Dad's room.

"They won't let you," Sam warned.

"I have as much right to ask Mr. Benson what price he wants as to look up the cost of a bike in a catalogue." She bumped into Dad's new waterbed and sat down hard on it, so the water sloshed away from under her. Clinging to the frame with one hand to keep her balance as the bed rocked beneath her, she groped for the phone on the bedside table.

Since there was no stopping her, Sam got the Bensons' number from information. It was long distance, so they had to keep the call short. All the same, Sam was surprised when his sister said, all in one go, "Hello, Mr. Benson, would you take six hundred and forty dollars for Tweed?"

"Who's this?" asked the farmer.

"Kate Linbert. I'm calling long distance."

"Oh, the girl that was here Monday? And you're offering six forty? Well, I suppose so. Let me speak to your mother."

"Oh, I'll be speaking to her myself. We'll call back to confirm. Thanks very much." She hung up quickly, flushed with embarrassment and triumph.

"Was that yes?" asked Sam.

"He said he supposed so, and that means yes."

"Well, I'd like to hear you get Mum to say she supposes so." Sam stuck his feet into his father's shoes and tried a few steps in them. They weren't all that much too big for him any more.

"We'll talk her round once she's got over the hassles about the well," Kate said confidently.

"What do you mean, *we*? I don't want her yelling at me. It's your money and your funeral."

"Be a sport, Sam. I'll give you equal time on Tweed for free, if you'll help me look after him."

He looked down at her. She was all fired up to carry through her grand scheme, and she needed her one and only brother to make the whole thing work. "Well, okay, I guess," he said. "I bet he'll end up being twice as much work for me as for you. But great inventors have to get used to working their butts off."

"Great. I knew you were sensible. You'll have a wonderful time with him, you'll see."

Their father called. "Sam! Kate! Time to go. Come and say good-bye to your grandparents."

"We see so little of our grandchildren," said Grammy. "Why couldn't we go with you for the drive and see the cabin?"

Oh no, thought Kate. If she sees the outhouse, she'll take us straight back to town.

"I only have seatbelts for four," said Dad.

"We don't mind, Dennis," said Grammy. That made Sam wonder whether her fussing about bike helmets came from concern for safety or a need to nag.

"Do you really think it's fair to Irene to turn up unexpectedly at this hour?" asked Dad.

That was the first time Kate had heard him

considering their mother in ages, and it touched her. Her mother's friends called him a selfish pig who walked away when he saw a female having a hard time. Yet here he was, standing up to his parents to keep them from interfering in the life the three of them were building up at the cabin.

Unless, of course, he was just making excuses to keep his parents from coming along as backseat drivers.

Either way, though, Kate felt closer to him. She decided to sound him out on the horse plot. She didn't quite know how to bring it up, though. They drove many kilometres down the highway in silence while she turned it over in her mind.

Finally she said, jerkily, "We're getting along all right at the cabin, Dad. Only there isn't much to do. So we were thinking of getting a horse."

"A horse? Is that your mother's idea?" He sounded amused.

"No, she hasn't agreed to it yet. But we've found a good horse and I can pay for him out of my own money, so I hope we can talk her into it. You've known her longest of any of us, Dad. How do you think we can get her to agree?"

Dad laughed. "Are you in on this too, Sam?"

"Yes. There's nothing sissy about this animal. The owner works with his horses installing telephone lines."

"Seriously, Dad, how would you put it to Mum?" Kate insisted, when she thought her father had chuckled long enough.

"Oh, lobbying is the same whether you're a kid pestering your parents or an admiral asking the government for a new submarine. Catch her when she's in a good mood, not worried by her in-laws. Tell her why you want the nag, say that it won't cost her anything and that you'll look after it all yourselves. If she says no, ask her politely why not and listen to her reasons. Then go and do something about them."

"Like what?" asked Kate.

"Suppose she says she doesn't believe the animal is any good, get an expert to vet it. If she doesn't think you can handle it, then prove you can. Are you sure you *can* handle it, by the way?"

Kate thought. "Yes. I have no idea how to prove it, but I feel this horse belongs at our cabin, and we can handle him. Or if we can't, then we can't handle anything at all, and we might just as well have him kick in our thick skulls."

"There's nothing much to looking after horses," said Sam. "Besides, he needs us."

"Well, tell that to your mother."

"But she said she didn't want to hear about any animal till we were all settled in, and she meant weeks, even months. Tweed may be sold by then," said Kate.

"Oh, don't despair," said Dad, with a touch of Grandpa's mockery. "She's into being a pioneer now, and a workhorse will suit her image."

"*You* don't mind us having a horse, do you, Dad?" asked Kate.

"No, but I'm not going to shovel up what it leaves behind." He laughed again. "Your grandparents will have a fit."

"Please don't tell them," Kate urged.

"Not if it matters to you. But they'll find out."

True, thought Kate. And they would insist that a horse was too dangerous and Kate had to be sent away to school before she killed herself with her wild ideas. Would Dad stand up to them? She was too afraid of the answer to ask the question.

It was dark when they reached the cabin. The faint light of one candle gleamed in a window. Dad pulled over on the grass but left the engine running and stayed in the driver's seat. He didn't say anything. Sam thought he was waiting for something. Kate just sat there, on the side closest to the cabin.

"Well, good-bye, kids," said Dad at length.

"What? Are we there?" asked Kate.

"Yes, come on. Good-bye, Dad," said Sam, opening his door and getting out. When he was tired he still forgot it was up to him to make first moves now.

"Which way?" asked Kate.

Her father switched off the engine and got out. She reached up and found his arm, then took his hand. She still couldn't understand how someone whose hand felt so large and warm and solid could sometimes be so slippery and icy.

"You should come in and see the house," she said as they walked up the hill.

"It's dark, fuzzhead," Sam told her. "You can't see anything by the light of one candle."

Mum came out to meet them. "Hello, everybody, did you have a good day?" She hugged Kate and Sam. She did not, of course, hug their father. Her voice cooled several degrees as she told him, "Your mother phoned."

Dad was turning to go already, but stopped to ask, also in a cold voice, "What did she want?"

"She *said* she was just calling to let me know you were on your way. But then she delivered a half-hour lecture on how irresponsible I am to be keeping the kids out of school. She wants specially qualified teachers for Kate, and piano lessons, and God knows what else."

"Just be grateful I didn't let her come along with us. She wanted to," said Dad.

"Maybe she should have. I don't think she'd have had the nerve to say all that to my face. Well, come along to bed, you two." She laid Kate's hand on the frame of the cabin door.

Kate shivered; the breeze on the hill was cold after sitting in the car. But she paused to ask, "When will we be seeing you again, Dad?" She still said seeing, because there really wasn't any other way to put it. She wished she had kissed him good-bye. But it was too late now, they were back with their mother.

"Maybe I'll come up Saturday, if it's not raining, and we'll look for a beach," he called over his shoulder. A moment later the car door slammed and he drove off into the night. As the noise of the motor died away, a cold stillness enfolded them.

6

Tweed by the Yard

Catching their mother in a good mood with nothing weighing on her mind was not going to be easy, Kate thought next morning. The well-driller had sunk a shaft thirty metres to get clean water. It could have been worse, but it could have been a thousand dollars or so cheaper. A large new electric pump lay beside it, waiting for the electrician to install it.

Late in the morning things brightened, for Mr. Hunt got a socket working. They were able to plug in a toaster oven and have grilled cheese without building a fire to heat up the whole cabin. Just as they were sitting down to it, the phone rang. It was an offer of translation work for Mum: a whole grammar of Inuit language, which would pay for the new well. She bubbled with pleasure as she bit into her sandwich.

"The only book that teaches you to speak the

language of the Inuit of Northern Quebec," she said, "was written in French by an old missionary. The government wants it translated into English. It's going to be a real challenge, but fascinating. The text will be ready for me tomorrow morning."

This happy mother sounded like as good a target for wheedling as she ever would be. Carefully, Kate said, "There's something I'd like to do with my bike money, Mum, if you don't mind."

"Oh yes?" she responded unsuspiciously.

"I'd like to buy Tweed."

"How can you think about a fall jacket in this heat! We'll look in August if you like, but there are none in the stores yet."

Sam laughed.

Kate replied, "No, I mean Mr. Benson's horse. I can pay for him all myself, and Sam will help me look after him. He won't cost you anything and we won't make any trouble for you."

"Hm," said their mother. "Do you both really want this?"

Sam shrugged and looked at Kate. The upper half of her face was too hard to read any more, but her mouth looked desperately hungry. He thought about galloping through the forest. "I guess so," he said.

Kate searched for words to express her intense longing without sounding ridiculous. All she could say was, "More than anything."

Mum considered. Then she said, "Well, your grandparents think you should have more to occupy your minds. They probably wouldn't approve of a horse, but it would teach you something, even if it didn't teach you all you're hoping for. We might get him on trial. But I don't think we should commit ourselves without consulting somebody who knows horses. Suppose we ask a vet to look him over."

Sam rushed to the phonebook to look up a vet before she came to her senses. When Mum called up and actually said in her best business-like manner, "I'd like to have a horse vetted," Kate was so excited she grabbed the back of the stairs and swung from them. She had never dreamed it would be so simple.

It wasn't. Mum hung up and said, "The vet charges a hundred and fifty dollars plus X-rays and mileage, and he can't come till next Thursday. I wonder how much they're asking for the horse."

When Kate told her, she laughed. Then she said, "Up at the general store I saw a blacksmith's business card — it caught my eye because it was a woman's name. Maybe we could ask her to help us."

The smith, Jenny Dale, was free that evening and would be pleased to look at a horse with them for twenty dollars.

Kate and Sam spent the afternoon in a fever, inspecting the fenced-in field and worrying that their mother would get cold feet. But at seven o'clock, with their feet only too hot inside their rubber boots, they drove down to the store on the highway, where Jenny the smith was waiting for them in an old van. She had long brown hair like Mum's but without any grey. In a slow, gentle voice, as if they were strange horses she had to calm down before she tackled their feet with a knife, she said, "Remember, I'm not a vet, I can't tell you about his wind and heart. All I'll be able to say is whether he moves all right."

"What I really want to know," said Mum, "is whether he's safe for the kids."

"That's not so easy to tell. All horses have their little quirks, things that make them mad or scared, just like people. He could seem sensible but freak out at running water, or mailboxes, or men in yellow raincoats. But we should be able to tell if he's a hard-core lunatic."

Jenny began by running her hands down Tweed's legs, lifting them up, and looking at his feet. "He could do with a trim," she remarked, and Mr. Benson said he'd been meaning to get around to it. After watching Mr. Benson lead him up and down the lane, she asked, "Would you care to ride him for us?"

The farmer laughed. "My riding days are long gone. We don't even have a saddle. But he'll carry you bareback safe enough."

Jenny vaulted lightly up. Tweed took a couple of very bouncy steps with his head high in the air and his ears twitching. Then, seeming to decide she was all right, he walked forward with long, swinging strides, his neck arched like a rocking horse. He carried Jenny into a large field dotted with bales of hay, and they trotted in and out between the heaps. Then they cantered round the edge of the field, Tweed's legs flashing under his belly.

"What are they doing?" asked Kate eagerly.

"Running around the field," said Sam. "He can really go!"

On the far side of the field, Jenny pulled up suddenly, then galloped on. She rode back to them and halted right in front of Sam. There was a dark, damp patch on Tweed's neck. Jenny swung down to the ground. "You can tell he hasn't been worked for a long time. He listens all right, though. One of you hop aboard."

Sam and Kate both stepped forward.

"Maybe Sam should go first," said Mum.

"But it's me that's buying him," Kate asserted.

Mr. Benson said, "No reason you can't both get on at once." He boosted Sam up, and there he sat, amazingly high, with his legs stretched as if he was straddling a chair. Only this chair had bones in surprising places and moved under him like a tire swing gone wild. He clutched the mane by instinct. He expected the same reaction as when he pulled a handful of his sister's hair — that is, she flung out her arms to hit him, jerked her head away and shouted "Leggo!" Tweed, however, didn't mind. Once Sam was settled on his back, he stood still, and then Kate was lifted up. The arms she clasped around Sam's middle quivered with excitement.

Tweed reached his head around and touched Sam's foot with his nose, sniffing him curiously. "It's like a riddle for him," said Sam. "What has four legs and weighs the same as one man? It's the Great Samkate."

Jenny led them along the lane at a walk. A jumble

of feelings went through the two riders. Is it really safe up here? How funny it is to have four feet walking under you and none of them your own. Sam felt like a general leading a parade, or a knight at a tournament, or a sheriff riding through a frontier town — like anything but the low man on the family totem pole. Kate felt she was being rocked by a big, strong, kind friend who wasn't going to run away from her or bawl her out or worry about her Future. She might not be safe from falling, but she felt supremely safe from the poisonous things that really bothered her.

When they turned into the hayfield, Jenny handed the reins to Sam. "Steer his head gently in the direction you want him to go, and push him toward it with your leg. If you want him to go faster, squeeze with both legs. When you want him to stop, pull gently on the reins and hold him with your back."

To take them left around the first pile of hay bales, Sam tried pulling on the left rein. Tweed's head came round and he stopped short. Sam dug his legs in to get him going, then tried steering his head left again, and this time remembered to push him away with his right leg at the same time. Soon he had the hang of it, and they were weaving between the bales in fine style. He tested the braking system a couple of times, and it worked fine. It was great to have all that power right under his control.

Then Sam pressed harder than ever with both legs. The walk became quick and jerky. Sam squeezed till his eyes felt about to pop, and Tweed broke into a trot. They laughed because it felt so funny, being tossed into the air. But the landings on that bony spine were no joke, and they were slipping sideways. Sam hauled on the reins, and Tweed slowed to a walk.

"Trotting is a lot easier with a saddle," said Kate.

They rode back to the gate, where Mum and Jenny, dark figures against the low sun, were swatting mosquitoes. "What's your verdict?" asked Mum.

"Thumbs up," said Sam.

"Make that four thumbs," said Kate.

"Will it be worth your life savings, Kate, and half an hour of chores every day, Sam?"

Kate felt her brother's shoulder blades wiggle as he shrugged them. "Yes," she said firmly.

"All right, then. Jenny says he's a good horse for you, for the price. We'll give him a try. But only for the summer, mind. If I don't think this is working out, then we sell him again at the end of August. Mr. Benson has kindly agreed to take him back then. But it's for me to decide if he stays or goes. Understood?"

"Understood," said Kate and Sam.

"You can have his bridle for twenty dollars," said Mr. Benson.

"Okay, I'll treat you to his headgear, kids. What else do we need?" asked Mum.

"A hoof pick, currycomb, and brush," said Jenny. "And you'll be safer and more comfortable with a saddle, and so will Tweed. We have to be careful not to let his back get sore from too much riding before his muscles get in shape. Twenty minutes at a time is plenty for him now, mostly at a walk."

"Sounds as if we have to go shopping before we can take delivery," said Mum. "Could you bring him over tomorrow afternoon, Mr. Benson?"

"I'd rather do it this evening, since you're here. Loading him into the truck isn't a one-man job."

In fact, there was work for three of them. Jenny took the leadrope and Mr. Benson went behind Tweed to keep him from changing his mind. Then they had Sam show Tweed a carrot and walk into the truck with it. Tweed followed him up the plank and took the carrot from him, and Jenny tied up the rope.

When Kate heard the rumble of hooves on the truck's metal floor, her heart pounded almost as loud. She took the six hundred and forty dollars from her purse and Mum counted it out to Mr. Benson. And with that, Kate became the owner of a horse.

Then they set off, with Mr. Benson leading the way and Tweed peering round at their car. They drove slowly along the rough, twisting road, and Kate had time to take in the changing scents as they passed new-mown hayfields and dense cedar bush.

Her dream was coming true. She had acquired a pair of eyes and the strong body and willing heart that went with them. That was certainly what she wanted and needed more than anything in the world. Even better, the horse plainly needed to be needed. They would be partners, with Sam of course, and learn all kinds of fascinating things together. She gave a deep sigh of happiness.

Yet there was a catch in her throat. Partly because at that moment they were driving through the sharp smoke from the everlasting fire at the township dump; but also because there was a catch in all the happiness she'd been expecting from her horse. For however much she might enjoy stroking him and being carried by him and looking after him, there was still the naked, terrible fact that she wasn't able to see him. Would probably never see any graceful, sleek, long-necked, slender-legged, wholly enchanting equine again in the whole of her life. Normally she managed to avoid such thoughts, but now, when she had confidently dared to say to herself, "There now, aren't you as happy as you ever dreamed of being?" she had to answer, "Not really."

The catch took those deep sighs and turned them into sobs. Kate felt a tear slide down her cheek. She buried her face in her arms and huddled down in the back seat so no one would notice her, because she certainly didn't want anybody to think she was sorry to own the splendid Lord Tweedsmuir.

Nobody did notice. Both Mum and Sam were still dizzy from the shock of this large animal careering into their lives. Mum said to Sam, "You're sure you checked all around the fence and he can't get out anywhere?" Sam vowed he had gone over it post by post.

They drove up the last hill and stopped. Down clanked the tailgate, then down the plank rumbled four hooves. A neigh rang out across the quiet hillside and echoed off the crumbling barn.

"Yes, it's all yours," Sam told him. "Nobody is going to shout you down here."

Kate wasn't sure that was what Tweed had been asking. She thought the neigh meant, "So where are all the other horses?" She said firmly, "You're going to like it here, Tweed. We'll take you out for a ride every day. Will you lead me to him, Mum?"

Her mother took her right hand and set it on Tweed's neck. The other hand joined Sam's on the leadrope. Together they walked him to the field, and Sam undid the old car seatbelt that closed the gate.

Tweed looked at the new world being offered to him. The grass was long and green, sprinkled with daisies, buttercups and purple vetch. He tore up a great mouthful and chewed it thoughtfully, gazing out of his great, wide-set eyes at the new people in his life.

All four of their minds, thought Kate, were full of questions they couldn't yet answer for each other. Tweed couldn't even ask his. But she would do her very best to find the right answers for them all.

7

Stumped by the Pump

The bicycle swooped over the rocks and leaped across the brook, landing with a light bounce on a bed of bright green moss and immediately coasting up between the silver birches. There seemed no limit to what it could do — Kate thought of flying right over the treetops with it. But it was, after all, only a dream, and there was a reason she would presently remember not to go on dreaming . . . something that had made yesterday wonderful and would make today even better. She let her dreams slip away so she could grasp at the knowledge, and there it lay, solid and real and worth all the dreams that had ever hovered round her pillow: her own dapple grey was just outside the door.

Quickly she rolled out of bed and pulled on her clothes, not bothering with the glasses because today it somehow didn't seem to matter what anybody thought of her face. She ducked under the curtain to Sam's room. That was a bonus of being blind: nobody minded you butting in on them before they were dressed.

"Sam, are you awake? We've got a horse to ride."

From Sam the only answer was a yawn, but from outdoors came a loud neigh. It was the most wonderful sound she had ever heard: her horse responding to her voice.

"It's not even light yet," Sam complained.

"There's got to be *some* light, the birds are singing," Kate insisted.

"They must be night owls," growled her brother. But she heard his bare feet slap down on the boards.

They found Tweed waiting at the gate for them in the dew-pale grass. "Is his water bucket empty?" asked Kate.

"It's fuller than last night," said Sam, and sloshed a handful of mosquitoes out.

Sam hadn't paid attention when Jenny was putting on the bridle, and couldn't figure out what went where. Kate found it hard to explain to him, but in the end she slid the bit into Tweed's mouth by feel, and Sam pulled his ears through and buckled up the straps.

For Kate to give Sam a leg up was fairly easy, but for her to climb up behind him was not. "You're pulling me off," he said. "I'll ride over to the cabin, and you can use the front steps for a mounting block."

Kate kept her hand on Tweed's shoulder for

guidance round the prickly gooseberry bushes. "Keep clear of the well and the pump," she reminded Sam anxiously.

"We're nowhere near the well, and I don't even *see* the pump. Hey, that's funny. They left it right there. Mum!"

There was no answer from inside the cabin. Sam looked around. It was a long way down to the ground and Kate was on it. He told her, "Go tell Mum it's gone."

Kate set off in nearly the right direction, and soon bumped into the steps and found her way into the cabin. Tweed tried to follow her, craning his long neck through the doorway. If he had been able to wedge his shoulders into the opening, the gallon of maple syrup might have drawn its sweet life to a sticky end. Luckily, only his head would fit.

That, however, was more than Mum was prepared for on first opening her eyes. She sat up in her hammock with a jerk, stared into Tweed's soulful eyes as if he were a dinosaur, and barked, "Get that animal out of here."

"But Mum, the pump's disappeared," said Sam.

Groaning, their mother climbed out of the hammock. "If Lord Tweedsmuir will kindly let me through . . ." Sam tugged on the reins and Kate leaned on Tweed's chest, and together they persuaded him to back out of the doorway. Mum followed them in bare feet to the place where the pump wasn't.

The grass lay flattened, but whatever tale it might tell to Sherlock Holmes, to them it said nothing. "Maybe Mr. Hunt needed to do something to it," said Mum. "But it's funny he didn't tell me. I'll call as soon as it's a civilized hour. If you're going for a ride, wear your bike helmets."

With helmets on their heads and mystery on their minds, they set off westward along the road. It was chilling to think a thief could have come while they were asleep, crept right up to the cabin, and taken what he wanted from under their noses. But they refused to let that distract them from the pleasure of exploring on horseback.

They rode around the bend in the road and came to the tree that marked the end of their land, an enormous evergreen like a living, sighing skyscraper. You could build a whole log cabin out of its timber, Sam thought. Its hundreds of green branches waved upwards as if it shook its fists at the sky and laughed, "Send me blazing sun, send me frost, send me thunderstorms, I don't care. I've got a built-in pump that will serve me no matter what anybody does to me." Sam decided to climb that tree some day soon, just to let it know it was his.

The road led through the forest for a long way. Birds woke and sang them on their way in many melodies. It took a great effort to remember Jenny's warning not to overstrain Tweed's back. When they turned around to face the risen sun, they made a pact: "Some day we'll explore this road to its very end."

Mr. Hunt said he hadn't taken the pump, so Mum called the police. Once they heard the address they sounded depressed rather than interested. No detective was sent up to take fingerprints from the grass or look for suspicious tire tracks. All Mum could do was order a new pump.

When Jenny came to trim Tweed's feet, she listened with sympathy to the pump story, and said, "This place used to belong to the Pippards, didn't it? They live up on the next line now. Anything left lying around within ten miles of them has a way of sprouting wings in the night. They haven't been caught red-handed, but for guys with no money they drive some pretty fancy wheels. Serving his time for burning the farmhouse didn't teach Joe Pippard anything good."

"Are they dangerous?" asked Mum.

"Not when they're sober," said Jenny.

This wasn't very reassuring. But Kate had so many questions for Jenny that she could spare no time for crime. Should they oil Tweed's hooves? Did he need extra minerals? Was trotting harder on his back than walking?

When Jenny had answered these questions ("once a week would be good, give him a salt block, and yes if you overdo it so get a saddle"), Mum asked hers. "Do you really think Kate can handle riding? Even apart from the safety, I'm afraid she may find it terribly frustrating to have a horse and yet be able to do so little with it."

Kate didn't always find it comfortable to have a mother who understood her.

"Well, time will tell," said Jenny. "One or two

coaches have done wonders with blind riders. Even taught them to jump, with a walkie-talkie on their hard hats so the coach can talk them over the fences. But I don't know of a coach who would come up here to teach you."

"I can't start paying for riding lessons," said Mum flatly.

Jenny shrugged. "Put her on the lunge line so she can at least learn to balance herself." So a lunge line and long whip were added to the shopping list.

"Like shopping for a new baby" was how Mum described their trip through the feed store and tack shop — an unexpected, adopted baby picked up on a few hours' notice. All the special equipment for feeding him, keeping him clean, and taking him for outings filled up their little hatchback so there was barely room for Mum's new translation, which was supposed to pay for it.

Tweed was waiting for them at the gate when they came to show him what they had bought for him. He sniffed their purchases over with polite interest. The salt block he welcomed with open mouth, but the currycomb found some ticklish places. He did appreciate the body brush, though. Kate spent a long time after supper grooming all over his coat and working the tangles out of his mane and tail. When she went to bed, her fingers still held the feel of his soft hair and the warm skin under it, the clean, hard bones of his legs and nose, the pillowy hollows of his flanks.

The lunge line, when they introduced Tweed to

it next day, was a complete puzzle. The idea was that Sam would stand in the middle of the field holding the long lunge rein and brandishing an immense whip like a circus ringmaster's while Tweed went around him in a circle. Since neither of them had ever seen a lunge rein before, however, Sam soon looked like a fork with a very long strand of spaghetti wrapped around it, and Tweed dangled at the end like a cheese-coated meatball, his ears twitching warily as he grazed.

Tweed had guessed that a pull on the line meant "Come here," and had walked trustingly up to Sam. The boy had waved a great snaky thing in his face to drive him away. So then he had concluded that the boy was inviting him to a tug of war, and he had thrown his energy into accepting the invitation like a good sport. Tweed had won the tug of war fair and square, but the boy had not taken defeat like a sportsman. After picking himself up and dusting himself off, he had waved the whip and shouted "Whoa!" — a total contradiction if ever Tweed had seen one. At that point he gave up trying to understand what the boy wanted and went for a tour of inspection around his field, while the little fellow trotted after him and jabbered incomprehensibly. Now Tweed had stopped to eat, and to wonder what weird thing these people would do next.

"Why are we doing all this, anyway?" asked Sam, throwing his whip to the ground and trying to step out of the coils of nylon webbing.

"So I can trot and canter by myself while you steer him," said Kate. "But he doesn't understand.

How about if you get on him and ride him in a circle around me, to show him what it's about?"

Kate felt silly standing with the equipment in her hands but having no actual control. All she could do was listen to the footfalls and feel the line moving, and turn in a tiny circle to keep up with it. But at least she had some notion of how to juggle the line and whip, since she had seen it done at camp. Fortunately Tweed had learned voice commands from the Bensons, too. Before long, Sam and Tweed both got the hang of it. When the children traded places, Tweed continued to walk around in an even circle like an old hand. Then Sam cracked the whip and Kate squeezed to make him trot. Relieved to be told something he could understand, he stepped out smoothly with his neck arched, swinging his quarters in rhythm.

This was Kate's first solo flight, and it felt good. She was bouncing happily with a light hold on the front of the saddle, trying to remember the jelly-belly trot she had been taught last summer, when Dad arrived for his Saturday visit. He parked in front of the field and came straight up to watch. To show off, Sam tugged on the lunge rein and said "Hoo-oo" to slow Tweed down, then gave his whip a really masterful liontamer's crack. Tweed scooted into such a fast, jerky trot that Kate nearly sailed off him.

"Boost me up in front of Kate and we'll take you for a tour, Dad," said Sam.

"Is there really room for both of you up there?" asked Dad.

"Yards of room," said Kate.

"You bought your Tweed by the yard, did you?" Dad chuckled.

"That's right, I bought him in the Bensons' back yard," said Kate. "And we keep him by the yard, beside our house."

Riding double, they took Dad as far as the monster pine, and then it was time to rest Tweed's back and put him away. Dad drove them to Joe's Lake for a swim. It had no real beach and the bottom was so rocky that Kate did no more than sit in the water to cool off, but there was a baseball diamond where Dad and Sam played Frisbee.

They picnicked on the grass at the foot of a weird, undercut sand cliff. Dad had brought along a book of lightbulb jokes, and Sam tried them out on Kate. They made up some Ottawa jokes together: "How many public servants does it take to change a lightbulb?" "Sorry, we can't tell without a Royal Commission." "How many auditors?" "One point three nine, with tax." "How many RCMP officers?" "Sorry, that's classified information."

As they were driving back, Dad said, "Some weekend we might go on a camping trip."

"But what about Tweed?" said Kate.

"You don't have to if you don't want to," said Dad, sounding hurt. "I thought you'd like it."

"Yes, we'd love to, but we couldn't leave Tweed for two whole days."

"When you've had him for more than one day, you may find it's easier to tear yourselves away," said Dad, with a touch of sarcasm.

Kate was sorry to see their happiest visit yet with Dad turn sour. "It isn't just that we'd miss Tweed. He needs us to look after him," she explained. "If we start leaving him to Mum, she'll make us get rid of him."

Sam said, "We could take Tweed on the camping trip, too. We could ride him to a campsite and you could meet us there with a tent, and we'd picket him for the night."

"Like cowboys under the stars," said Dad. Maybe he was still being sarcastic — it was hard to tell with him.

"Or knights errant," Kate agreed.

"Only there isn't much open prairie hereabouts," Dad objected. "And I don't suppose provincial parks let you use them as barnyards."

"But the beach at Robertson Lake is practically empty," said Sam. "We could tie him to a tree and let him graze."

"We'll see," said Dad at last. "If you're still as keen to take Tweed on the road after you've had him another week or two, we'll talk about it. But it would take a lot of organizing."

"I can do all the organizing we need," said Sam positively.

Kate wondered where he had got all this confidence, and what kind of trouble it would lead to. She found it strange that her accident had not shaken her little brother's faith that accidents were things that happened to other people.

8

Tweed by the Bolt

Sam soon decided a two-day trail ride and campout was too tame and began to plan a three-day trek for the upcoming long weekend. In a county map, he discovered a promising trail that followed the line of the old lumber railway into the back country. It passed along a chain of lakes including Robertson and Flower. He shared his find with Mum and Kate right away.

"Don't ask me, talk to your father," said Mum. "My translation is due the first of that week. I'll have to work right through the holiday, so I don't have time for any camping trip."

A car screeched past the house. "Wow, they must have been doing a hundred and forty," said Sam.

"Good thing you're not out riding, with those guys on the loose," said Mum.

"Would you read to me, Mum?" asked Kate. She

was oiling Tweed's bridle, and she didn't want Mum worrying about the dangers of the road.

"I suppose it is time for a break," said Mum, and picked up a battered *Huntingtower*, which had caught Sam's eye in a second-hand shop beside the laundromat because it was written by Tweed's namesake. Like their own companion, Tweedsmuir the writer brought secret dreams to life, and carried you with him at a breathless pace while somehow making you feel safe. The tale captivated their mother, a bookworm to the core. An author could fire her heart when the noblest and friendliest of horses still couldn't do anything for her but make her slightly nervous. Kate heard her voice humming with excitement as she read how the hero pored over his map and staked out the wild hills of Galloway.

"Those hills aren't far from Lammermoor, which the little place way down this road is named after," said Mum.

A little more of this, thought Kate, and we'll have her ready to go exploring with us, walking beside our own Tweed.

Sam looked out the window while he listened. A distant roar from the direction of Lammermoor warned that the car was coming back. It rocketed into view, a big purple machine with a raised rear end, all wheels and engine. Just past the cabin it screeched to a halt. Sam saw two men staring at the cabin — large, bristly-chinned men in peaked caps, shouting something they couldn't catch.

Mum stopped reading and came to look.

"Do you think they know we're here?" asked Sam.

"Our car is there to tell them so, even if they can't see in," said Mum, locking the door.

"Who are they?" asked Kate.

"Some young toughs, and they sound pretty drunk. Maybe the people who took our pump have drunk the proceeds."

A barrage of bottles came flying out of the car and crashed against Tweed's fence. Tweed neighed in alarm. The men laughed and gunned the engine, and with a great roar the car drove away.

"Did they hurt Tweed?" cried Kate.

"I don't think so, but we'd better clear the glass up before he cuts himself," said Mum. "Bring that cardboard box, Sam."

"Why don't we call the police?" asked Sam.

"I don't suppose they'd drive all the way up here just to give a speeding ticket. And there's no sense making those men mad at us for reporting them."

The bottles had shattered into hundreds of fragments that played hide and seek among the long grass. Tweed came over to help, and looked hurt when Sam shooed him away.

"We ought to train Tweed like a guard dog," he said. "He could fight really well with his hooves and teeth."

"Don't you go turning him into a dangerous animal. I don't want him trying out karate chops on us."

"Then what about a dog?"

"Oh, I don't know," said Mum crossly. "I came up here to lead the simple life and get some work done to keep the wolf from the door. I don't want to be bothered with more livestock right now, hooligans or no."

Next morning, on their ride, he tackled Kate on the problem. "We really should have a dog to deal with those hooligans. Are you getting a seeing-eye dog or aren't you?"

"I don't know," said Kate. "They don't usually let you have one until you're seventeen. Till then your parents are supposed to be your guides. But depending on where I end up going to school, I may need a dog eventually."

"The real way to scare bad guys off," said Sam, "is with a gun."

"Mum wouldn't go for that at all."

"I know," said Sam moodily. "Don't hold on so tight, you're pinching me."

"Sorry. To feel really safe . . . I don't know about you, but I wish Dad was living with us."

"I know." They usually avoided talking about this. "It doesn't look as if he's coming back, though."

"I'm not so sure," said Kate. "I can't believe he's really happy with Cynthia. She's way behind him in brains, she never understands his jokes, and she's no fun. She pushes him around more than Mum ever did, sending him for haircuts and making him take his clothes to the cleaners. And he didn't let Grammy and Grandpa meet her. I bet he's ashamed of her."

"Yes, but getting fed up with her isn't the same as coming back to us," Sam pointed out.

"I suppose not. Mum talks as if she doesn't want him back, too. But since we managed to talk her into letting us have a horse, I've been thinking maybe . . . well, once he gets this Cynthia thing out of his system, maybe we could talk Mum into letting us have our father back on the same terms as Tweed: provided we make sure he behaves himself and we keep him happy."

"You're as bad as Cynthia. Dad is too smart and too pig-headed for us to manage."

"We don't exactly have to *manage* him. We just have to show him he can be happy in our family. He left because we were all miserable —"

"That wasn't *my* fault," Sam interrupted.

"Why can't you talk like a civilized person?" Kate exclaimed. "Yes, the accident was my fault, but it could have happened to anybody. Maybe it's been hard on you, but it's been a lot harder on me, so don't rub it in. Splitting up was Dad's decision. If we'd been easier to live with, though, he might not have gone wandering off. I'm not saying we can turn into perfect people and have him fall all over us, but I do think that if we stop sniping at one other and show we can look after ourselves and have fun together, then maybe he'll have the sense to come back to us."

Sam rubbed the side of his head. "That thing you're yelling into used to be my ear. Hey, there's a snake!" He halted Tweed.

"Where?" asked Kate anxiously. She had never

been keen on snakes, and not being able to see them made it worse.

"It was on the road but it slithered up the bank into the woods." He peered down into the leafy shadows.

"Did it have rattles?" asked Kate.

"Sh!" Sam swung his leg over Tweed's neck and dropped to the ground. Into his sister's hands, which were clutching comically at the air where his waist had been, he thrust the reins. Stealthily he crept up the steep bank that overhung the white gravel road.

"What *are* you doing, Sam?" asked Kate. She didn't like being alone with Tweed in case a car came by. She would hear it coming, but she wouldn't know how to get out of its way, and the road had so many bends, the driver might not see them until it was too late. Some of the people who used this road might even think it was fun to drive right at a horse and scare it off the road. Even if no cars came, she was afraid Tweed might step into a ditch. He was strangely fidgety this morning.

It was not until later that she connected the fidgets with the tense seatbones poking into his back and the nervous clamp of her legs around his ribs. She didn't want to think how their angry voices might affect him. She could barely remember when Sam was a squalling infant in a baby-pack, who drove people frantic because they couldn't tell what was bothering him.

The snake was a real beauty, Sam saw: midnight black with amazingly bright yellow stripes running its whole length. Not a rattler's pattern, and there were no rattles on its tail. With a quick lunge, he caught it.

The creature writhed in his hand, its scales as smooth and dry as the leather reins come to life. Girls thought snakes were yucky and slimy, but this animal was as wonderful to touch as to see. Sam looked at his squeamish sister, sitting on what she thought was the only good animal in the world. "Give me your hand," he said.

She gathered the reins in one hand and reached out the other, thinking he needed it to mount. It was taken not by a firm hand clasp but by a finger — a weirdly double-jointed finger that bent back over her hand and wriggled all over like no finger . . . She shrieked. A snake was crawling up her arm! She shook her arm wildly and dropped the reins. The snake slid down Tweed's shoulder and wrapped itself around his leg like a fireman sliding down a pole.

That was too much for the bravest horse. He tossed up his head and bolted. Kate was thrown off balance and grabbed at his neck to save herself. She had no idea where the reins were and she had slipped too far to have any hope of clambering upright again, but still she held on by sheer will-power until she was sure they must be well clear of the snake. Then she gave in to the wrenching pain in her hands and fell to the gravel.

Sam stopped laughing. The look on Kate's face when she realized she was holding a snake was priceless. But when the horse disappeared in a cloud of dust and his sister lay in a moaning heap, the price of that joke began to look steep. He ran to her, calling, "Are you okay?"

"Catch him before he runs into a car."

Any car, thought Sam, was a lot likelier to run over a huddled-up girl than a large white horse. He dragged her by the arms to the side of the road. "Stay put, I'll get Tweed," he told her.

He ran along the road, following wide-spaced hoofprints. With a stride that long, Tweed could be running loose on the highway by now. If Tweed caused an accident, Sam would be in water hot enough to power a steam engine. The sweat dribbled into his eyes as he sprinted down the winding road.

Kate's hip and side were aching hard, and she had skinned her elbow on the gravel. But what made her sickest was worry about Tweed. If anything happened to him, she wanted blood. That boy was like their father at his worst, not caring who got hurt so long as he could have his fun. Men had no sense of responsibility.

"It's all right, I've got him," she heard Sam calling.

Kate started to sigh with relief, but her ribs were too sore. "Is he hurt?"

"Not a scratch. Just sweaty."

Kate heard the even footfalls of four hooves and a pair of sneakers. She rose painfully to her feet, but she wasn't sure enough of the footing to walk toward them.

"I'll give you a leg up," Sam offered.

"Why should I trust you after what you put in my hand?" she demanded.

"I'm really sorry, Kate, honest. I meant it as a joke."

"Some joke," sniffed Kate, but she let him boost her up onto Tweed again. "How are you going to get up?" Once she was on her horse, it was easier to be generous.

"You're sure you want me?" Bright red drops were dripping off her elbow, and an ugly lot of gravel was ground into her arm.

"Well . . . it was the dumbest joke I've ever heard of, but we can't all have a superb sense of humour. If the noble Lord Tweedsmuir has forgiven you, I will too. Come on up and help me walk him cool."

Sam led him to a bank that overhung the road in a miniature sand cliff. It was awkward getting on in front, because he had to swing his leg high over Tweed's neck, but he managed it. If he rode behind Kate he couldn't see where they were going.

"So, about these parents," said Kate. "We need to get them talking to each other again. This camping trip may help because it will take so much arranging. Mum and Dad both spend too much time staring at computer screens. All that hardware hardens their hearts. Nothing straightens you out like a long hike — if you can't ride, that is. If we could get them out to Flower Lake together just once, they'd start turning into sensible human beings again."

Sam wasn't entirely convinced, but he didn't want to start another argument.

What Kate told Mum when they got home was that Tweed had stepped on a snake and scared himself. So Sam got off with only a warning to steer clear of snakes. Their mother shook her head and wondered out loud what trouble that dumb animal would land them in next. They had to remind her she'd given them until August to prove they were safe together.

Next day the replacement pump was finally installed, and Mum burned energy at her computer to pay for it. Sam and Kate rode Tweed for a little longer every day and grew steadier in the saddle. Tweed gradually converted his field from a wilderness of long grass to something like a lumpy lawn.

Sam had hoped to go over the route for the camping trip with Dad on the weekend, but Dad spent the whole time in Montreal with Cynthia. Sam and Kate, remembering a breathless gallop around the aquarium and the rides at La Ronde, wondered why Cynthia rated two days in Montreal when they'd only had one, and that was two years ago.

Saturday it poured. They rode Tweed in raincoats with a towel over his back, but the damp on his hair soaked right through their pants. After half an hour of that they sought shelter in the cabin. All the mosquitoes in the township had had the same idea. They swatted mosquitoes while they finished off *Huntingtower*. Then they began to yawn with frustration.

Their mother said, "Be thankful we're not Inuit living in a tiny snowhouse with a howling blizzard outside, and no sunshine for three whole months."

"What do they do to pass the time?" asked Sam.

"Dream up ways of making their language more complicated. They have nine past tenses and nine future tenses to say exactly what time they mean, so they're very aware of each passing moment. What they don't have separate words for is he and she. Talk about not discriminating on the basis of sex." Her voice went dreamy. Would her next move be to some far northern tundra where women and men were fully equal, Kate wondered anxiously.

Sunday they woke to the same steady downpour, warm and steamy as a monsoon. Even a snowhouse would have been a welcome change. Sam kicked the wall and shouted, "There just isn't anything to *do* here!"

"Let's go to church and meet some neighbours," said Mum.

The small brick church with the tall steeple was stuffy, as if the doors had been shut all week and the air left over from last Sunday was now being breathed by many sticky, overdressed people. The organ wheezed, and people seemed scared to compete with it by singing heartily.

The Gospel reading, however, would have riveted Kate to her pew even if the melting varnish hadn't. It was about a man born blind. The disciples asked Jesus whose sin it was that caused him to be blind, his own or his parents'. Jesus replied that it had nothing to do with anybody's sins; he was blind so God's power could be seen at work in him.

The preacher said it was easy to miss the full meaning of this because the man was promptly healed. "But the story shows Jesus meant more than that he had been made blind simply to give the Christ a chance to solve all his problems with a fancy miracle. When God takes away something we think we need, such as vision or the support of people we rely on, we may feel unable to carry on, and we may get bogged down in worrying about what made God angry at us. But really God is paying us a great compliment by saying, 'I know you can handle this, because I know what stuff I've made you of.'

"As soon as the man in the story gained his sight, he had to face a far harder challenge. The religious authorities pressured him to say he had only been pretending to be blind. They cursed him and threw him out of the community. His own parents abandoned him out of fear. But he still found courage to speak out the truth that this unknown man had opened his eyes. That is how God's power was seen at work in him, and how it can be seen in us, in the courage with which we face our challenges."

If God expected Kate to cope without sight or a resident father, He must think she was an amazingly strong person, she reflected. So where was all this power He was waiting to show in her?

She didn't feel any miraculous electric energy surge through her. After lunch, though, when Sam had gone to compare model planes with a boy he'd met at church, Kate asked her mother to show her how to use the computer. Mum set her fingers on the keyboard and told her, "Right middle, left baby, left forefinger up right, left middle up," and that was her name, K-A-T-E. After a little of this, her fingers began to remember the keys. With prompting from Mum, she typed a letter:

Dear Grammy and Grandpa,
Thanks for the dinner last week. Sam and I now share a very handsome seeing bike called Lord Tweedsmuir. We will send you a picture later. Don't worry, we wear our helmets. Everything is fine. I am typing this myself on the computer.
Love, Kate.

As Kate licked the envelope, she felt sorry for her grandparents. All the things they tried to force on her and Sam, from steak to bow ties, were intended to make the giver feel useful. Their message was, "Take this, you must need it, because we want you to need us." But they still weren't needed the way Tweed depended on Kate and Sam to give him water, to pick stones out of his feet, and to explore the wide world with him.

Put like that, it was surprising how many people didn't have an animal. Didn't they like being needed? Why not? Did it, perhaps, scare them?

Kate seemed to hear the echo of her father's big car driving away down the hill toward the impersonal, lonely city. He knew enough not to shower her with things she didn't need. But suppose what she did need from him scared him because it was too hard for him to give?

The more she thought about this, the more difficult it all became. It seemed that whenever something happened that made her feel good, such as mastering the computer, she immediately became aware of the problems that she had shut out of her mind while she didn't feel so buoyant. What could have made her father abandon the people who had been his life for so many years? She knew it couldn't be anything small and simple, like Cynthia having a prettier face than Mum. Something deep inside him must have been disturbed.

So how could she reassure him?

When the rain stopped and she and Sam were out splashing through the puddles on Tweed, she tried to share what she had been thinking with Sam. "You know, maybe we should rethink this camping trip, or scale it down to a one-day hike, with both parents if they'll agree. The way you have it planned now makes us too dependent on Dad. I think that's what really bothered him about what happened to me: it made me so helpless at first."

"Since when have you become super-competent?" asked the person who was steering her horse.

"I'm not. That's the point. When we're out in the wilds there will just be too many things I need somebody to help me with, like finding a place to go to the bathroom. He can't handle that. He could end up completely fed up with us. Besides, it's too dangerous, with all these pump-thieves and bottle-throwers in the neighbourhood. If something does go wrong while we're riding, Mum will think it's because of Tweed, and she'll make us give him up."

"Oh come on, Kate, you're being a real drag," said Sam. "If there was no danger there wouldn't be any excitement."

9

Bound to Flower

Early on the Friday afternoon before the August long weekend they finally set off on the great expedition, which was to take them over sixty kilometres. On the first day, Kate and Sam and Tweed would be escorted by Mum on her bike to Flower Lake, where Dad was to meet them in his car with a borrowed tent and their sleeping bags. Once they were with Dad, Mum would bike back to the cabin and her computer and leave them for the weekend. The farmer at Flower Lake had agreed to let Tweed share his cattle pasture for three nights. They planned to spend Saturday exploring the lake. On Sunday they would ride along the old Kingston and Pembroke Railway line (alias the Kick and Push) to suss out some more lakes. On Monday they would return home to the cabin by a different road.

The plan had been argued and bargained over to

allow each person most of what he or she wanted. Mum got a short outing on Friday but had the weekend to herself to work. Dad got three mornings to sleep in with no noisy neighbours. Sam had wanted to camp at Robertson Lake on the Sunday night, but the parents had vetoed that because it meant driving the tent over. Despite Kate's plotting, the parents had arranged it so they would be together only for the unavoidable half-hour at the end of the trip in which Mum would ferry Dad back to Flower Lake to pick up his car and the tent.

Exploring his hinterland in a real, continuous journey made Sam as fired up as if he were Champlain discovering it for the first time. Kate's misgivings were as strong as ever, but after all that Sam had put into this she hated to be too much of a spoilsport.

The narrow road glittered with white quartz gravel. They crossed Waddle Creek and wound through the woods, in which three or four cabins lay hidden. Presently their road ended at a wider thoroughfare of tawny dirt. Straight ahead it would take them in another two kilometres to the paved highway that led to Ottawa, but now they turned left to let it carry them northwest, deep into the Canadian Shield.

They began to sing "Northwest Passage", belting out the chorus. They were breaking new ground. Perhaps never before had a bike and a four-footed beast together struck out along this road. The last chorus brought them to a bridge over the Clyde River, a broad green current fringed with the purple loosestrife that was now setting the countryside on fire. Kate caught the scents of mint and watercress.

The saddle held both riders at a pinch — a persistent pinch that became annoying after half an hour, so they took turns getting off to walk. Kate dismounted now, and Mum got off her bike so she could push it by the handlebars while Kate rested her hand on the seat for guidance.

The road changed from a straight, flat concession line to a winding hill road. The woods drew in closer, farms became scarce and rough. A few old farmhouses still stood surrounded by their snake-fenced pastures and apple orchards, but other dwellings looked thrown together at random, claptrap mobile homes flanked with broken cars. Sam wondered if the people who lived there were too spaced out to care what they looked like. Did one of those scrap-heaps of rusted farm machinery hold the pump theirs was stolen to replace?

Soon the woods closed in around them completely, towering over them on steep hills. A small stream crossed the road on its way to the river. The trees drew back from it to form a narrow meadow gilded with black-eyed Susans. Here they rested, and let Tweed help himself to water and grass.

"This is exactly the kind of place John Buchan liked best in the world," Mum observed. "A secret, half-wild meadow enclosed by forest — he said this part of Canada and the Swiss Alps were the best places to find them."

"I wonder whether Tweed is really Lord

Tweedsmuir come back to life," said Kate dreamily.

"Whatever gave you that idea?" scoffed Sam.

"Well, *I*'d like to come to life again as a horse and enjoy my favourite countryside. To us it's picturesque, but who appreciates it more than Tweed does, eating it and rolling in it?"

Mum laughed. "Would you really rather be that kind of geegee? Buchan might have liked it, at that."

"Was he a rider?" asked Sam.

"Yes. At the end of the Great War, when he was all bruised and tired to death, he moved to the country and rode his horse every morning. That gave him his second wind, so he went into Parliament and became a GG and did everything he could to prevent another war. He almost succeeded, too, except he couldn't get the British and Americans to stop sulking at each other. So then he had to sign the declaration that brought Canada into World War Two. It was the death of him."

It struck Kate as terribly sad that whole countries would nurse their wounded pride and refuse to work together for peace. She thought of the way her parents kept sniping at each other. No, there didn't seem to be a way for outsiders to stop them.

"What do you mean? Did he really die of a broken heart?" asked Kate.

"He started to write a book about the places where he'd gone fishing, and fell into a trance, and nobody could bring him back. Maybe he just gave up on civilization and decided to haunt a place like this forever. But *we* can't. Come on, it's time to hit the road again."

The late Friday traffic had begun. Every few minutes, they were overtaken by a car loaded with fishing gear and towing a boat or sporting a sailboard on the roof. They raised great clouds of dust on the dry road.

At Joe's Lake, Sam said, "I feel like a roasted marshmallow that's fallen in the ashes. I wonder when Dad will come. He could be here soon, if he got off work by three-thirty. If we're lucky he'll get the tent all set up and waiting for us, so we'll have time to swim in Flower Lake before dark."

Mum said, "Somehow that doesn't sound like the Dennis I know."

After following the Clyde River, now broad and swampy, for a space, the road struck northwest again onto higher ground. The steep rise tipped Sam's weight back onto Kate. She volunteered to get off and walk, because her feet were growing heavy from dangling.

Near the top of the hill, Sam looked back and saw the river far below them. Beyond it stretched thickly wooded hills as far as the eye could see. He tried to make out their cabin as a distant speck, but it was far out of sight.

Another lake came into view on the left. "What a lot of lakes they have around here," exclaimed Mum. "What's this one called?"

Sam pulled the folded topo map out of his shirt front. "Widow Lake, the last one before Flower."

"Some omen," said Mum with a sniff. "I wonder what can be keeping your father. I'll have to leave you guys by seven so I can get home before dark. My bike can't make much speed on these gravel hills."

"Maybe he drove past while we were picnicking and we didn't see him," said Kate.

Their climb was rewarded by a long downhill stretch. Kate mounted and they let Tweed trot, with Sam standing in the stirrups and Kate sitting in the saddle while their mother coasted silently beside. Faster and faster they went, until they came to a sign saying "Flower Station". They reined in then and rode at a discreet walk past a cluster of houses and a tiny store. The Clyde was here no more than a young brook, crossed by a miniature bridge. A short way past it they crossed the old railway line they were to follow on Sunday, a narrow track leading into deep woods.

"Not far now," said Sam.

The road bent to the right, and there lay Flower Lake. Sam strained his eyes for a big blue Buick.

The closer they came, the less sign they could see of any dark blue car. The road led them right up to the lake, so close that the water was almost lapping the shoulder. A herd of red cattle grazed in a field that ran down to the water's edge. The road bent left to hug the southern shore. That was where they had arranged with Dad to set up camp, and he had promised to be there soon after five.

It was long after six, and there was no sign of him.

"I knew he'd leave us in the lurch again," said Mum bitterly. "Wait here while I ask at the farm if they've heard from him."

They dismounted to wait at the roadside and relieved Tweed of his saddle and bridle. Sam had barely snapped the halter on when the leadrope was jerked from his hands. In a moment, great gulps of lake were disappearing up Tweed's throat. "Hey, come back, animal!" shouted Sam.

Hearing his splashes, Kate was afraid. "Is he in the lake? Catch him, quick!" She ran toward the sound. The sudden resistance of water brought her up short. She realized how dangerous it was for her to plunge into unknown waters alone. The sound of her own sloshing on top of Tweed's (or was it Sam's?) disoriented her. "Oh, Sam, don't let him drown!" she pleaded.

"He's not drowning," said Sam as he ploughed through the shallows. The sandy bottom sloped very gradually, and Tweed stood knee-deep several metres from shore. Sam fished out the rope. Little lumps of water slid under Tweed's skin all the way up his neck. Then he pawed the bottom like a moose, drenching Sam and stirring up the waters into murk. Slowly and gracefully he sank to his knees and rolled over in the water, and the rope jerked out of Sam's grasp again.

Kate, hearing another exclamation from Sam and a noise like a giant washing machine running out of control, called, "What's he doing?"

"Pretending he's the Loch Ness monster," said Sam. What if Tweed swam off into the wild blue yonder? But there was no way to prevent him without getting in the way of those thrashing legs.

With a tremendous splash, Tweed rolled back onto his feet and stood up. Water cascaded off him in rivers. Quickly Sam seized the rope and wrapped it around both hands.

Tweed seemed to think he had done what he came to do. He followed Sam willingly to the shore. Once there, however, he stopped short. Sam turned to see what was the matter, and was caught full in the face by a blast like a firehose as Tweed shook himself.

When Mum returned, she demanded, "Hey, who said you could go swimming? And with your clothes on, too!"

Sam answered, "I didn't — at least, only second-hand. Tweed is a messy drinker." Quickly he changed the subject. "Did you track Dad down?"

"No," said Mum. "I called his apartment and got no answer. I even called Cynthia's. I don't know what we can do if he doesn't turn up at all. We can't go all that way back in the dark, but we can't very well sleep in the open without so much as a blanket, either."

They sat on the grass and thought of all the things that might have happened to their father. The longer they sat, the likelier the worst things became. Maybe he had crashed the car. Maybe he had just changed his mind about spending a whole TV-less weekend alone with his kids. Kate didn't know which she was more afraid of.

To pass the time, Sam pulled out the map and

checked it against what he saw. Though the map called it Flower Round Lake, this was no circular pond. It was only a little more oval than the finger lakes that squeezed into the narrow, glacier-carved valleys. From the small farm at the near end, the shore stretched away into steeper slopes lightly sprinkled with summer cottages. Over the far end loomed Clyde Lake Mountain, not a rocky peak but a high hill such as an energetic boy might tackle in an afternoon. This landscape appealed to Sam: wild but not savage, it offered everything he might want in manageable helpings. The lake was almost small enough to swim across on an ambitious day.

What a pain, then, that the tent that was supposed to be his base for exploring this country and the father who was to explore it with him were nowhere to be found. Would they have to turn around and go right home to spend another boring weekend at the cabin?

As the sky gradually flushed pink with sunset and they finished off their emergency rations of crackers, Sam and his mother flushed with annoyance. Only Tweed seemed unconcerned. The grass here was every bit as good as at home, and there were cows to make faces at. Kate listened to his contented crunch and thought, What's another disappointment so long as I've got my horse beside me? Mum, however, began cursing the flake she had married.

Kate wondered if she would ever not mind her parents being angry at each other. Possibly her hurt would dull in time, as the hurt of losing her sight had done, becoming just a set of practical problems to be solved one by one, with an ache underneath. Her parents acted as if they thought they shouldn't have got married, which meant no Kate and no Sam. Of course, they still loved Kate and Sam — at least, they said they did, and most of the time it could be believed. But Dad had just left their lives so — easily. Whenever Mum told them sharply to stop goofing around, Kate listened for the sound of her tolerance cracking under the last straw. Some day Mum too might run away, to some equal opportunity snowhouse. Sam would turn into one of those pale, pock-marked creatures that haunted video arcades. Dad would still invite her over for the odd Saturday evening in front of the invisible TV, when he wasn't doing the big city with Cynthia. But the rest of the time, Kate would be confined to Grammy's residential school for the visually challenged, where she would cane the seats of uncomfortable chairs while her four-footed soulmate faded into a distant memory.

"Do you really hate him, Mum?" asked Kate in a low voice.

"Of course not. Would I have lived with him fifteen years if I could hate him? I just despise him. As long as the sun shines, he's witty and charming, but let one thing go wrong and he wimps out totally. He dreamed up this trip to prove he was a tough wilderness man, but now he's faced with the real prospect, I bet it's too much. The trouble is, his parents brought him up to think that if he looked good and impressed the neighbours, that was all that mattered, he didn't need a sense of responsibility. Guiding your sister, Sam, and taking care of that horse have made you more of a man than your father ever was."

Sam didn't know what to say. People didn't usually have the insight to pay him such compliments. He felt proud but also uneasy, as if he were wearing man-sized pants over a pair of stilts. Trying to live up to his role, he suggested, "We could make a shelter out of branches for the night."

He pulled out his pocket knife and sized up the nearest trees. None of their boughs looked especially yielding. He was not sorry to be interrupted by Kate saying, "I hear a car."

They stood up and watched the dust cloud, but their hopes fizzled when a little mauve sportscar sped into view. The car jammed on its brakes, and Sam exclaimed, "Hey, that's Cynthia's car!"

Their father stuck his head out the window and asked, "Is this where I park?"

The cool question drew a hot reply from Mum. "You're more than three hours late. What on earth have you been up to?"

"My car broke down and I had to borrow Cynthia's. She was invited for the weekend to a cottage south of Perth, so I dropped her off there first. Then I tried to take a back way here, but the signs were wrong."

"You mean you got lost," said Mum. "And now I'm stranded here for the night. Why didn't you phone?"

Dad got out and began unloading the trunk. Clearly he wasn't going to say "Sorry I'm late."

With an effort, Kate said, "Hello, Dad, I'm really glad you're here," and smiled, hoping his back wasn't turned to her.

"Hello, kids. Give me a hand with this tent, Sam."

Sam pulled the tent out of its bag. The flapping canvas startled Tweed. What was this large, noisy thing wrestling with Sam? He trumpeted to scare it away.

"I'd better settle Tweed into his field," said Sam.

"But we need to pitch the tent before dark," said Dad.

"I'll do the tent, you look after your horse," said Mum.

The cattle all turned their heads to watch Sam and Tweed approach their field. They stared out of black eyes in heavy, neckless heads and stepped slowly but purposefully toward Sam. As he undid the chain on the wide gate, he pictured all those shaggy red beasts making a dash for freedom and mowing him down. He hustled his excited horse through the gate and slammed it behind him. As soon as he had turned Tweed loose, he hustled out again and chained the gate, saying, "Good luck, pal."

Tweed trotted up to a large cow and touched noses with it. For a full minute they stood face to face in silent conversation: the new kid in the schoolyard squaring off with the oldtimer. Then

Tweed cantered to the fence and tore right around the pasture, bucking spectacularly. When he had done the full circuit, he put his head down and helped himself to grass. The cows stood well back and gaped at him.

Sam found his family were not settling in as peacefully.

"Why on earth didn't you find out how to set up the tent when you borrowed it?" Mum exclaimed. "And I can't believe you left the kids' air mattresses behind on the cabin steps."

"I couldn't fit them into the car. Hand me that peg, will you?" said Dad.

"Here you are. It's not safe to leave the cabin unoccupied this long anyway, and a pile of things on the steps for everyone to see makes it worse. There are too many dishonest people around."

"Is it my fault you've chosen to live in a high-risk area and have inadequate security?"

"You know perfectly well that's all I can afford."

Kate, who had been conscripted as a tent pole, stood with her hands full of canvas and thought how nice it would be to lie down on something soft.

By the time the tent had been persuaded to stand up by itself, it was far too dark to ride a bike. No one felt up to making a campfire and cooking over it. They sat in the dark, opened a couple of tins of tuna and argued about who should sleep where in the three-person tent. Somebody would have to sleep in Cynthia's car. They expected Mum to, because the camping trip was supposed to be for father and children. But Mum disliked Cynthia too much to want to be cooped up in a metal box that smelled of her perfume and cigarettes. So Kate stretched out on the narrow backseat with her sleeping-bagged feet sticking out the window.

After a few minutes on the hard ground in the tent, which smelled as if it had spent the winter in a damp basement, Sam heard the front seat calling to him in a soft, thickly padded voice. The handbrake between the bucket seats jabbed his ribs when he lay crossways, so he made the passenger seat recline till it was almost resting on Kate's knees.

He settled back as if he was in a dentist's chair. A few mosquitoes imitated the whine of a dentist's needle. Oh yes, he'd forgotten to brush his teeth, but so had everyone else. He drifted off to the muffled sound of his parents whispering through dirty teeth.

10

Marooned

A kick in the head woke Sam. He opened his eyes and sat up with a jerk. A scrap of paper fluttered in front of him, stuck under the windshield wiper: "See you Monday night. Have fun! Love, Mum."

He turned around and saw Kate wriggling like a frenzied worm inside her sleeping bag. "What did you kick me for?" he demanded.

"Sorry, just getting my swimsuit on. Come for a swim?"

"It's too cold."

"Maybe, but my hair got caught in the ashtray. Come and keep an eye out for sharks, please."

He gave an elaborate sigh. "I guess I have to. Mum's gone away."

"I know, I heard her," said Kate. She had hoped that their parents, penned up together in a small tent, would somehow sort out their differences.

The sound of Mum pedalling away had been a sad awakening.

The water was as still as ice and as exhilarating as the first snowfall. Its tingling peace washed the sadness out of her. Kate resolved to take hold of that morning calm and make it last through the day.

Tweed trotted up to his gate to see them, cheerful and caked in dirt. They brushed off most of it and promised to take him out for a ride after breakfast.

That was not their father's idea, however. When he finally got up, yawning, and rustled up a breakfast of cereal and long-life milk, he was in no hurry to set off exploring. He built a campfire and heated water for coffee. Halfway through his second mug, Sam spread out the map in front of him, expecting it would set his father's feet itching the way it did his. But Dad seemed content to hold the map and gaze blankly at the view.

It was a pleasant view, with the lake all hazy and the morning sun brightening the hills on the western shore, but Sam had had a good eyeful of it the evening before in the long hours of waiting. A horse was now champing at the bit for him.

"The real way to explore this country," Dad began, and paused for another mouthful of coffee, "is by canoe. West of here there are no roads at all for fifty kilometres, only an endless network of lakes and rivers. You take a light canoe, birchbark for choice, and you could paddle and portage for days without meeting a soul, like the old furtraders."

The only time they had rented a canoe, it had gone round and round in small circles and collided with the dock. Sam, who was very small at the time, had laughed and begged for more, but Mum had refused to allow either of them in a canoe with their father again until he had perfected his J-stroke. As far as the children knew, he hadn't wetted a paddle since. Another case, their mother would say, of his wimping out of anything challenging. He would rather sit on dry land and lecture about the fur trade.

"It was lumberjacks who really opened up this area," he went on. "They spent the winter chopping down trees . . ."

"Why winter?" Sam asked, as his father paused for more coffee.

"Because that's the easiest time to get around, when the trees are bare. Just strap on your snowshoes and you can walk over the lakes and through the bush."

"And their horses could haul the logs over snow better than mud," Kate added.

"Yes, then in spring, when the melting snow swelled the rivers," Dad continued, "they floated the logs down the Madawaska River and into the Ottawa. Later they shipped the lumber out by train, along the line we'll be following tomorrow."

"What about following it for a bit in the other direction this morning?" suggested Sam.

Dad shook his head. "We have two days of solid hiking ahead of us. Let's do some scouting in the car first."

They didn't argue with him, feeling that enough arguing had been done already. Anyway, Sam looked forward to his first drive in Cynthia's car, which was new and expensive and loaded with gadgets. Sam wondered if it was the car that had attracted his father to Cynthia in the first place. It was the one thing Sam really liked about her.

They followed the road around the lake and up the slopes along its western shore. For such a new car it gave a very bumpy ride, thought Kate, or maybe the road was just too rough. Sam got Dad to stop so they could look at the lake, now a deep blue under the clear sky. The uninhabited far shore lay green and peaceful.

It was when they were getting in again that Sam noticed the flat tire.

"Of all the God-forsaken places to have a breakdown!" exclaimed Dad. Other times when they had had a flat, he had phoned the motor league. Now they had no phone, and the motor league was miles away. Groaning, Dad dug into the trunk for the spare tire.

It was no easy job. Even to figure out how to assemble the jack, Dad and Sam had to puzzle over the instructions in the owner's manual, which was written in translationese. But the real trouble was loosening the lugs that held the tire in place. Kate listened to her father grunting and cursing in the dust and thought they had been wrong to go ahead with this trip, they weren't up to it. But they were caught in it now, and she could do nothing.

Suddenly Dad crashed the wrench against the fender so hard it chipped the paint and dented the bare metal. "This useless wrench is too short," he snarled.

"Shall I see if I can borrow one with a longer handle?" Sam offered.

"I guess you'll have to. Otherwise we'll have to get towed to a garage with an air gun, and heaven knows where there'll be one open today. But I can't leave the car here till Tuesday."

Sam ran to the nearest cottage and found no one. The next cottage had no tools except a screwdriver. Deciding his best bet would be the farm, he jogged down to the lakeshore, shutting his sweat-bleared eyes to the lure of the cool lake.

The farmer lent him two wrenches. Then, thinking of the long, hot, uphill climb and the impatient Dad at the end of it, Sam got Tweed out, tied the leadrope to both sides of his halter and climbed off the fence onto his bare back.

Meanwhile, Kate sat beside the car and tried to keep the morning freshness of the lake from ebbing away from her memory. If only she could *see* the lake. Maybe she could get her father to let its cool beauty in through his eyes to refresh them both.

"What's the view from here?" she asked.

"Oh, a lot of water, a couple of million trees and half a dozen cottages. There's a cedar A-frame that looks like a smaller version of the one Cynthia's staying in now. That's a real gem, with cathedral ceilings and stained glass. Must have cost them a bomb. Bedrooms galore — there's quite a crowd staying for the weekend. She'll be able to get a lift back to the city with somebody if she wants. I sure hope I can get that dent touched up before she sees it, or she'll nail my hide to a fencepost and never let me near the car again. That's fifty bucks down the tubes at least for the paint. Plus patching the tire."

Eyes can let in only what you're willing to take into your mind, thought Kate. If *she* had eyes to focus on Flower Lake, she surely wouldn't fill her mind with pictures of scratched metal and a raving Cynthia. But she tried again. "What colour is the lake?"

"Blue, of course. You don't get green lakes in the Canadian Shield, because it's all old, hard rocks like granite. The Rockies, now, are younger, and the rock dissolves and gives you emerald lakes. Wish we had something to drink. I don't suppose there's a cold beer between here and the highway. What I wouldn't give for one."

This man, thought Kate in despair, is always ready to lecture you on geology or history. But what button could you push to get him to look at a beautiful thing and enjoy it? He wasn't programmed for that. It must come of being brought up by Grammy, who took you to the gallery to look at paintings of lakes and forests because paintings count as culture, but didn't understand why you wanted to live in the middle of the real thing, visible or not.

For Mum, culture and history were the stories of real people's struggles and loves. She understood what delighted the Inuit or John Buchan and what frustrated them. Perhaps that went with being a translator, getting inside people's skins and speaking with their voices. But it had also burned away her natural defences so that people got under *her* skin and stung her into snapping at them.

Just as Kate was wondering if perhaps her mother was right, and the only way to make her father notice the lake was to tell him to go jump in it, her ear caught a distant hoofbeat. Her heart leapt. "Is that," she asked, "a knight galloping to the rescue on a white charger?"

"I believe it is," said Dad, with the beginnings of hope in his voice.

Bless you, Tweed, she thought, you'll be the saving of us yet.

Bareback and with one hand full of tools, Sam had to stretch his legs long to keep his balance as he cantered up the road. Tweed was having such a good time he didn't want to stop, not without a bit in his mouth. Sam hauled his head around toward the car. They screeched to a halt with Tweed's knees almost touching the bumper.

"Try these," he said, handing the tools down to his father. "If they don't work, Tweed can give you a tow."

But Tweed's hidden talents as a draft horse were not called on. After a few more grunts and only one or two curses, the wheel came off. Shortly a proud father said, "Now you can get back in."

Kate decided it was time to put her foot down. "Thanks, but I'd rather take the white charger." She was sorry if Dad's feelings were hurt, but she had had all she could stomach of that car of Cynthia's.

Sam announced, "When we get back to camp, I'm taking Tweed straight into the lake to cool off."

Tweed's trotting feet made a terrific splash until the water rose to their toes. He kept on, straight out to sea, even when the water rose above their knees and they felt his feet leave the bottom and begin swimming. They floated off and swam one on each side of him, with their hands in his mane.

"You look like you're having fun," called Dad from the shore.

"Jump in and join us!" cried Kate.

He did. They dared him to play tag. The three of them together could swim faster than he did, but they were slow in turning, and Dad ducked out of their way at the last minute toward Kate's side, where there was no one to see him. Soon Tweed caught on to the game, however, and followed Dad like a polo pony chasing the ball. Kate felt Tweed's neck turning in her direction and knew Dad was in front of her, so she swept her arm wide and tagged him. He gave a deep laugh.

Then it was their turn to run away. Kate dug her fingers firmly into Tweed's mane and kicked for all she was worth. They surged through the lake, twisting like sea monsters. But suddenly, strong arms closed around her waist. Shrieking, she tried to cling to her horse, but her hold was broken.

Dad squeezed her tight against his hairy chest, then let her dangle loose by one arm. "One down, two to go," he said, and launched off again, dragging Kate behind him. This lake, she decided as it shot up her nose, had done almost too good a job of washing the starch out of her citified parent.

Hunger eventually lured them out of the lake.

After they had eaten and Tweed had gone back to join the cattle, they were surprised to see Mum drive up.

"What's the matter?" Kate asked her.

"I've had a call from Cynthia. She insists you bring her car back right away, Dennis."

"But you can't, Dad!" exclaimed Sam.

Dad turned not to him but to Mum. "What exactly did Cynthia say?"

"She wants you," said Mum wearily, "to bring the car back tonight to the cottage where she's staying, because she intends to drive down to Syracuse tomorrow and shop. You can either stay with her or have her put you on the bus to Ottawa, she says."

"But she lent it to me for the weekend," said Dad.

"She's changed her mind," said Mum. "I told her the kids had been counting on this camping trip for weeks. She just said that's too bad, it's her car, and I shouldn't be a sore loser."

"I have to think about this," said Dad. He sat down on the hood of the car and stretched out his legs. "Tell me, kids, what would happen if I went back to Ottawa and left you?"

"But the camping trip was your idea in the first place," Sam protested. "It's not fair to ditch us in the middle."

"I was only asking what would happen *if*," said Dad. "Could you two kids handle riding home by yourselves tomorrow?"

"I guess so," said Sam, but he didn't sound too sure.

Kate said, "If Sam fell off and Tweed got loose, I couldn't do much to help."

"No," said their mother firmly. "Too much could happen to them. With three, you have one to stay with a casualty and one to go for help."

"I hope you didn't tell Cynthia I'd call her back right away," said Dad. "You would, though, wouldn't you? Trying to set me up for a fight."

Mum flared up. "You haven't learned a thing in the twenty years I've known you. Whenever you see trouble brewing, you run away. When will you realize it never works?"

"Listen, Irene, couldn't *you* ride shotgun for the kids?"

"No way! I am under contract to finish six thousand dollars' worth of work by the first of the week. I'm wasting time right now carrying your floozy's messages, and you ask me to sacrifice a whole day. Well, I can't afford it. *I* take my commitments seriously."

Kate and Sam shifted uncomfortably. Their instinct told them, when a parent was raving, to keep their heads down. But Kate knew that was precisely what drove her mother furious. Maybe she should try her hand at peacemaking, even if her head got bitten off.

Dad began in a tone of icy sarcasm. "Let me remind you . . ."

When he paused for effect, Kate leaped in. "Dad, you only need the car to get you back to Ottawa in time for work on Tuesday, don't you? So Mum, if your work has to be delivered on Tuesday, you could take Dad to the city Monday night and he could deliver it. Let him take Cynthia's car back to her now, and you follow him and drive him back to us here, and then go home and work. We'll just carry on as planned."

Nobody said anything for a minute. Kate wondered if they were going to yell at her for butting in.

"How far away is this cottage?" asked Mum dubiously.

"Less than an hour," said Dad. "I have to be in the office first thing Tuesday morning. Will you be finished by then?"

"If I have two clear days with no more interruptions, I should have the job wrapped up by suppertime Monday."

"Right, then," said Dad.

"Good thinking, sis," said Sam, much relieved.

Their expedition was saved.

When the mauve sportscar had driven off with the blue hatchback behind it, Kate and Sam settled down with Kate's new deck of cards, which looked ordinary but had braille markings as well. She was beginning to master the system, and Sam was learning it too so he could do blindfold card tricks.

The sun was low and birds were flying home to their nests when Mum drove back, with Dad in the passenger seat, and parked beside the tent.

"Sorry we took so long," said Mum. "We stopped at the cabin to pick up the air mattresses. Is everything okay here?"

Kate and Sam assured her it was.

"By the way," Mum asked, "how many single mothers does it take to change a lightbulb?"

Sam thought of saying ten, to tease her. But since she had been so helpful, he co-operated by asking, "How many?"

"Even if a single mother could *afford* a new lightbulb, when would she ever find the time to screw it in? Think of me chained to my computer, and remember to enjoy yourselves extra for me."

"We will," said Kate.

Mum kissed them and left in a cloud of dust. Kate was dying to ask Dad what they had said to each other on the drive. Instead she asked, "What did Cynthia say when she saw the car?"

"Oh, she went on about the dent, even though I offered to pay for it. Also she complained the whole car was filthy and stank like a pigsty, and there were white horse hairs all over the leather upholstery. I started to dust it off, but she said that wasn't good enough, so I left."

"Did you tell her she has no spare tire now?" asked Sam.

"Heavens, no. If she gets a flat on this trip, I'll have to move house."

His children laughed. "Good thing you've got the tent," said Sam.

"You're not very sympathetic, are you? Just like your mother."

Kate wondered if Cynthia knew about the night he'd spent in the tent with Mum. But Cynthia had at least seen Dad drive away with Mum. If her aim in demanding the car back had been to test her power over him, she couldn't be happy with the results.

"So here we are, marooned without a vehicle for the next two days. We'll just have to hope there are no emergencies. Think you can handle it, kids?"

"We'll do our best," said Kate.

11

Cloudburst

The Kick and Push trail was narrow even for the back country, because it had been a single track line. But what it lacked in breadth it made up in depth: a rock-solid foundation carried the miniature railbed straight across the middle of swamps and over hills. As they rode through the Sunday morning calm, Sam pictured old fire-breathing, steam-spewing monsters hauling giant logs at speed through the wilderness.

The track ran high above Widow Lake, dropped down to a swamp where it was carried on a series of little wooden bridges like a rustic Venice, then climbed up into the heart of the forest. Wildflowers waved them onwards: a golden stretch of black-eyed Susans, purple loosestrife, bristly blueweed and cheerful chicory. The sweet clover grew so tall that Tweed snatched mouthfuls as he passed without even bending his neck. Right beside the trail, beavers had gnawed down a stand of trees. They saw a beaver dam blocking the South Clyde far below.

Into the silence broke the roar of a labouring engine. A fat camper van squeezed its way slowly down the track. They climbed up among the stumps to make room for it. The monster caught its tail against a tree and knocked loose an aluminum lawn chair strapped to the back. The chair dragged along the gravel, but the driver seemed not to notice its clatter over the roar of the motor as he drove away. Dad waved at him and pointed, but in vain.

"Silly fool, that chair will be knocked to pieces," Dad remarked. "That's what comes of taking everything but the kitchen sink when you camp. People don't realize it isn't how much you can carry with you that counts."

"No, it's knowing how to enjoy what you've got," said Kate.

"And knowing where you're going," said Sam.

"And who you're travelling with," said Kate. She smiled at her father, or at least at where his voice had last come from. It was one of her not-so-minor frustrations, not to know if her smiles were landing in the right spot or if they were returned.

She wondered if, when he said it wasn't what you carried with you that counted, he was talking just about camping or about life in general. Since he had surprised them by moving out, she had never been sure she understood what was in his mind. How could you tell what mattered to him except by what he carried with him? To judge from the things he filled his apartment with (not to mention the things he left out, such as beds for his kids), you would think all he cared about was yuppie comfort. If he was really saying none of that counted, that was exciting. But maybe he meant something different, and maybe when she said what counted was who you travelled with, he didn't realize she meant she wanted to travel with him, wherever he was going. Or maybe he didn't especially like travelling with her, because she wasn't enough fun.

She would have felt much less secure if it weren't for the large, steady horse carrying her. She reached back and patted Tweed on the croup, grateful that horses responded to pats, not smiles. At least there was someone she could get through to as well as anybody else could, if not better.

"Your turn to get off and walk, Kate," said Sam.

Unfortunate but true. She slid to the ground. Her father's long stride kept going. He seemed not to have heard, or to have forgotten she needed guiding. She would have to ask him to take her hand.

Somehow that was more than she could do, to ask him to hold her hand, and then carry on, knowing he was only touching her because she'd asked him to.

If she could catch up to him and take his hand without having to say anything . . . But he was getting farther away. If she ran after him, she might fall on her face and make a fool of herself.

She stepped forward instead in the direction of the hoofbeats, reached out and touched warm horseflesh. With her hand on Tweed's croup she could follow without getting in the way of his feet.

For ten kilometres they walked and rode without seeing a single dwelling, until they came to a couple of isolated old farms. They picnicked on the shore of a broad, shallow lake, where there was no sound but wind and bird-calls and gently lapping water. They could have been a hundred years back in time, and a thousand kilometres from any city.

By the time they got back to camp it was evening and they were tired to the bone. Sam and Kate took Tweed into the lake for a drink, while Dad started rustling up supper. Before he could get the fire lighted, however, he ran out of matches. As if that were not enough, the can opener broke.

"Shall I borrow one from the farmer?" asked Sam.

"I hate to bother him again," said Dad. "Maybe you'll have to borrow a can opener, but I'll see if I can buy matches at the store in Flower before it closes."

"Leave Tweed here," said Kate. "His feed is ready for him, and he's earned it."

So while Dad headed for the store and Sam for the farmhouse, Kate held Tweed by his leadrope and listened to him crunch his oats. She told him how well he had behaved, as she felt his legs for signs of strain. They were as slender as her own, yet they stood up to phenomenal pressure. He was so fragile as well as so strong. That was why she loved him fiercely.

Tweed finished his oats and moved on to grass for his next course. A strange sound grew in the air, like an airplane engine but rougher. The leadrope jerked in Kate's hand. "It's all right, Tweed," she said. The noise grew until the air throbbed with the chopping of helicopter blades directly overhead. The leadrope was torn from her hands.

"Tweed! Come back! I won't let it hurt you!"

She had no idea where he had gone, because the helicopter drowned out his hoofbeats. A cold fear went through her. Tweed was loose, and who knew where? This was his great chance to make a dash for freedom, whatever that meant to him. Home, back to his mother and sister on the farm where he'd been raised, in the next township. "Stay with me," she pleaded.

There was no response. The helicopter passed on into the distance, and silence fell. She strained her ears. As far as she could tell, she was alone.

What if Tweed had caught his legs in the rope and broken them? When would Sam and Dad come back? She felt completely helpless, not being able to see even a hoofprint to tell where Tweed had gone.

"Tweed, best beast, please come back, if you can."

A warm nose butted her shoulder.

"Oh, bless you!" Kate said, and threw her arms around her horse's neck. The leadrope was dangling free. She coiled it up and planted her hand firmly on Tweed's shoulder while he grazed, so that she could feel his every movement.

"Thanks for sticking around, Tweed. You're a real pal." She gently kneaded his crest. Every human she knew except her mother, and Sam so long as nobody else was watching, felt uncomfortable with her because she couldn't see them. The accident had been like a magic ring that made people invisible to her, and it scared them. But she was already so different from Tweed in so many ways, in how she walked and what she ate and how she shared her thoughts, that the difference in sight seemed small and unimportant. He didn't mind being invisible to her any more than she minded him not being able to read her letters. What mattered was that they cared about each other and looked after each other, each in their own way.

Next morning they said good-bye to Flower Lake and the campsite that had been their home for three nights, and set off on their last and longest journey.

At first they followed the road they had come by on Friday. At Joe's Lake, they turned up another dirt road, which rollercoastered up past three or four old farms until it seemed to reach the top of the world. They were completely alone in the woods, with no sound but rustling leaves. Even their footfalls fell silent on the cushion of pine needles, which gave off a sharp, fresh smell. A deer stared at them, and let them come quite close before turning its white stern to them and bounding away. The sun sparkled on a distant lake, but here they were shielded from it by a canopy of green.

Without warning, Tweed planted all four feet on the ground and raised his head. His nostrils flared, his ears pricked and his whole body quivered. "What's the matter?" Kate asked him.

"I can't see anything," said Sam.

"Listen, there's something coming on our right," said Kate, stroking Tweed's flanks to reassure him.

Something large was crashing through the undergrowth. A man, thought Sam. But what emerged stood the same height as himself. It looked disconcertingly like a boy who lived on doughnuts, never trimmed his nails, and wore his mother's fur coat. The eyes, though, were tiny, black, and totally wild. It lumbered across the road and vanished noisily into the bushes on the other side.

Tweed leaned against the reins, as if he thought this was no place to linger. Agreeing with him, they hurried on.

"You're hardly safe down there on the ground, Dad, with bears around," said Sam. "You should get a horse."

"Give me a break," said his father. "There's enough on my plate already: two children, two women. How come you want to saddle me with a horse as well?"

"Get rid of one of the women," Sam grinned.

"A horse might be less trouble," Dad admitted.

Toward noon, they came to the county road. They turned left, with their backs toward Robertson Lake. This road was wider and more open, and the sun beat down on them from a clear blue sky scattered with wisps of cloud like Tweed's tail. By the time the travellers came to the village of Poland, a half-dozen houses that seemed like a metropolis after the long stretch of empty bush, they were ready to pounce like hot and hungry bears on the general store's ice cream cones. Kate chose vanilla so her dribbles wouldn't show on Tweed.

The air hung hot and heavy over them as they

left Poland and pushed on through the woods. Heavy clouds rolled up and the sky darkened ominously. Eight more kilometres lay between them and the cabin. They trotted and Dad jogged until his shirt stuck to him.

At last they came to their own Waddle Creek Road, leading down to the left between tall cedars. They hustled along it and dipped down to cross the Little Clyde by a narrow bridge. The light turned a peculiar violet. Thunder growled at them like a farm dog out for their blood.

"We aren't going to beat this storm," panted Dad, holding his side.

Black clouds gathered overhead and began to spit large drops of rain. A finger of lightning stabbed the earth two fields away, and a sharp crack rang out right after, making them all jump. Tweed jumped highest, since he had the most legs. Sam hauled at the reins, and Kate murmured reassurances.

"Get down, you're perfect targets for lightning," said Dad. They slid off, and Sam gave Kate the end of the reins to hold beside him, so as to guide her while keeping her clear of Tweed in case he spooked again. The rain poured down all at once, soaking their clothes.

"We'll wait it out in the next barn we come to," said Dad.

They plodded a long, wet, worrisome way without finding any barn. The lightning crashed overhead, and the road turned chocolate brown except under the dense cedar trees. Sam was tempted to crouch in one of those cosy dry spots, but he knew that under a tall tree was the worst place in a storm. It grew so dark that they could see only a little way ahead.

Slowly the thunder rolled away. At length it was no more than a distant growl like a bear slinking back into its lair. Then the rain slackened, the clouds parted, and the sun burst out to make every leaf sparkle. The air came alive with the new-washed scents of wildflowers.

Of all the roads they had explored, Sam felt this one had the most character. There were mature hardwood forests, abandoned farms with over-grown pastures, and one or two farms still thriving after a century. A huge white mansion rose grace-fully behind a private lake with islands joined by high-arched bridges, the work of an ambitious landscaper of long ago. A little farther they came to a tiny schoolhouse with a big bell, standing all by itself. "Too bad it's not in use, or we could ride to school next fall," said Sam.

As they turned the last corner, the sun shone directly behind them. Only a straight two kilometres of uninhabited woods lay before them.

"Will you look at those rainbows!" said Dad, pointing straight ahead. "There's nearly the full spectrum in both of them: red, orange, yellow, green, blue. Looks like the pot of gold must be right in your cabin. Isn't it pretty, Kate?"

He looked at Kate, and his mouth fell open. He mumbled something and turned away. Sam glared at him.

To cover the awkward silence, Kate started singing, "Somewhere over the rainbow, way up high . . ." She hoped they'd join in with her, but neither of them did. She carried on anyway, because she liked the song. She'd always liked singing, and in the last few months it had grown to mean a great deal to her, filling in the void left by not being able to paint. This was a girl's song, though, too sentimental for men to strain their Adam's apples with. She switched to something heartier just for them: "I Am a Happy Wanderer," in the version their mother sang when she washed clothes. Sam did join in for that, and then their father's tenor fell in below them:

> "I am a happy launderer, I love to soak and scrub,
> And as I wash, I love to sing,
> And sloosh things round the tub.
> Laundereee, launderaaah, laundereee,
> launderahahahahaha . . ."

That was much better. Kate liked it when her father was right there, sharing their craziness, instead of wandering through a maze of adult worries. Even in her wet clothes, she felt warm.

The light turned golden with evening. Sam's own particular monster pine came into view, hung with raindrops like diamonds set in gold.

Then at last Sam saw the cabin nestling into its green hillside. Tweed neighed in triumph. Agreeing with him heartily, the humans burst into cheers. "We made it! Sixty kilometres by muscle power alone!" cried Sam, and thumped his sister's back behind his own.

Mum came out calling, “Welcome home, travellers!” She took pictures of them looking bedraggled but victorious. Then she handed out towels and dry clothes. Sam came back from turning Tweed into his field to see Dad looking like a scarecrow with his ankles sticking out below Mum’s jeans.

“How are the Inuit?” asked Kate.

“Just the table of contents and I’m through,” Mum answered happily. “It will be a big relief. Some of the useful conversational phrases hit too close to home. I’m thankful *nanortaonennginavit*, that is, you weren’t eaten by the bear.” She smiled at Sam and touched Kate’s arm.

“So, Mum,” asked Kate, “do we get to keep Tweed for good? You said you’d decide in August, and we’re well into August now. Have we proved we can handle him?”

“I said the end of the summer. Don’t rush me. But I guess I have to say you’ve been doing awfully well with him. Unless you have a major disaster, I think he can stay.”

Tweed’s riders cheered so loud she covered her ears.

After supper, Sam went along with Dad in Mum’s car to collect the tent before dark. As they drove, Sam marvelled at how far they had ridden. He had dreamed this journey up out of his own head and a piece of printed paper. The force of his imagination had carried them through a real landscape of solid wood and rock and water, and brought them safe home. He stretched contentedly.

Beside him, though, his father manhandled the

gears and looked unhappy. Finally he burst out, "Poor Kate, she used to love rainbows and lilacs and all those things. I can't believe I forgot she doesn't see them now. I feel so *useless*."

Sam had never heard him talk that way. Did his father actually need comforting? "Kate's all right. She doesn't need you to give her a rainbow."

"But there's so much I want to share with you both, and I can't, and it makes me feel a failure, so I give up trying."

Sam wondered if this was a good time to ask for a bigger and better bike. Maybe not just yet, though. He said awkwardly, "Don't worry about it. Kate's happy with our horse. If she *asks* you for something, you could try to give it to her, I guess. But we have most of what we really need."

His father still looked troubled. Sam couldn't think what else to say. By the time they returned to the cabin in a fogged-up car full of wet tent and gear, night had fallen.

"So, are you ready to take me into town, Irene?" asked Dad.

Kate was sorry that just when they all seemed more comfortable together and prouder of one another than they had been for years, Dad was asking to go. "Can't you stay till morning?" she asked.

"I have to be at work at eight, showered and changed. We'd have to get up awfully early. Anyway, it looks pretty crowded here even without me." With their wet clothes draped from the loft, the little cabin looked like Noah's ark halfway through the flood.

Before this weekend, if Kate and Sam had seen Dad suddenly so anxious to leave, they would have been hurt. But after the long road they had travelled together, they were more inclined to feel sorry for him. They were at home and he was not. Sam almost felt guilty about being the man of the house. But it had been Dad who by leaving had forced them to find new ground to put down roots, and grow to fill his place. If he wanted to change that, he would have to make a move.

Mum said stiffly, "I'm ready to go when you are."

Dad's good-bye hug was a brief, tense grip. Kate's heart ached for him as she listened to them drive away.

A few minutes later they drove back. Kate's heart leaped: Dad had taken the plunge!

But only Mum came up to report. "The storm knocked down a telephone pole. The road is blocked, and the phone must be dead. We'll have to go round by Lammermoor. I'd feel safer taking you along, but the wet tent pretty much fills the car. Besides, you need your sleep."

"We'll be fine here," Sam assured her, yawning.

"Well, don't open the door to *anyone*. I'll try to be back in two hours."

The dangers of being alone in a remote cabin with no phone were not enough to keep people as tired as Sam and Kate awake and worrying. Their foam mattresses seemed the height of luxury, and they turned their faces to their own solid log walls and were asleep within seconds.

12

Tweed by Miles

A powerful engine was coming toward them. Kate woke first. "Mum, are you home?" she whispered.

There was no answer. She ducked under the curtain and shook Sam gently by the shoulder.

"Whazzat?"

"Sh. There's a truck coming up the hill. I hear men talking in it."

Sam crawled out to the edge of the loft and looked down. The truck backed up until its tail lights were right at the cabin door and stopped with the lights off but the motor still running. Someone shone a flashlight through the front window.

Kate whispered, "How will we know if it's safe? Can you see them?"

"Not yet," said Sam. "They may think nobody's here, since there's no car."

The door rattled savagely. Then a heavy blow

was followed by splintering. Someone was trying to break the door down with an axe!

Their hearts stood still. Then their brains began to work furiously. They grabbed each other. Sam whispered, "We'll make a run for it out the back door."

"We'll ride Tweed and hide in the woods," said Kate.

Trying to make no noise, they slipped down the stairs while the axe struck again and again. The whole house shuddered under its blows, and the thin panel door split like kindling. While Sam fumbled with shaky hands at the bolt of the back door, Kate felt for the bridle hanging on its nail and clasped it tight to her.

The bolt yielded to Sam's hands with a loud click. There was a pause in the axe strokes. "Hey, I hear somebody inside," said a rough male voice.

Kate and Sam tumbled out the back door and ran toward Tweed's field, tearing through the tall grass and bushes as fast as they could. In the pitch dark, where sight was no use and they had to rely on memory, Kate forged ahead. Sam got tangled in the branches of a young pine tree. The man with the flashlight ran around from the other side of the house and shone its beam on Sam, who was trying to beat his way through the tree. The man jumped on Sam and caught his arms.

Sam yelled and fought for all he was worth, kicking out wildly. The man was so strong that he held him pinioned with hardly any effort. He laughed, and didn't even cover Sam's mouth or tell him to be quiet. Sam burned with humiliation and yelled even louder, calling him all the names he could think of. But it was useless to call for help. Having no neighbours to hear when you shouted your lungs out was not such a piece of luck as he'd once thought.

When he paused for breath, he heard the distant creak of Tweed's gate opening. So Kate had made it to the field. He was about to call to her when it struck him that the thugs hadn't seen or heard her. It was up to him to cover her getaway. He roared as loud as he could and kicked at the bushes.

He was amazed at how much noise he could make when he really put his mind to it, letting loose all his fear and anger. The thug lost patience and shouted, "Shut up!" but Sam kept going, even though his throat began to hurt as much as his twisted arms.

Then the man with the axe came out of the house. Sam hollered harder than ever. The axeman said something he couldn't hear over his own noise. Then he bellowed right in Sam's ear, "Belt up, you!" and made as if to hit him with the axe. Its head was as broad as Sam's face and it had a very serious blade that glistened in the beam of the flashlight. Sam shut up, like a radio switched off.

Over the rumble of the truck engine, hoofbeats were dying away into the distance. If you weren't listening for them, you might not know what they were. Was Kate aboard, or had Tweed run away by himself in terror?

The first man picked up the flashlight, which had

dropped to the ground when he first tackled Sam. They looked him over. Sam stared back. They might have been the same men who had thrown the beer bottles at Tweed from the car after their pump was stolen, but he couldn't be sure, because they had stockings over their faces. They stank of drink.

"So what do we do with the little rat?" asked the flashlight man.

"Tie him up," said the axeman.

The flashlight man dragged Sam to the panel truck, threw him on his face in the wet grass with the exhaust flooding his lungs, and knelt on his legs while he tied his hands behind his back with strong rope and then tied the rope to the back of the truck. "Don't move!" he ordered. Then he switched off the engine.

There didn't seem to be much choice for Sam but to lie there. He listened to the men helping themselves to the valuables, starting with the computer. He was so furious he could almost cry. He was also very uncomfortable, with the rope biting into his wrists, the dew soaking through his pyjamas, and sharp things sticking into him through the grass. Something really vicious was biting into his ankle. He felt for it with his toes and it stuck between them. It felt like a bent nail, probably thrown away by the men who had built the shelter for the pump.

On impulse, Sam transferred the nail to his fingers and wriggled until his back was against the rear wheel of the truck. He could hear the two men indoors ripping the woodstove out of the wall.

Surely that would hold them for a few minutes. Sam jabbed the nail hard into the sidewall of the tire. It went in so far the skin of his fingers tore pulling it out.

A stream of air blew strongly against his hands, like a hundred-year-old giant blowing out all the candles on his birthday cake. The hiss was drowned by the clatter of stovepipe falling to the floor and china shattering.

Sam's heart rose to his mouth as the men came out of the house. But the cast-iron stove was so heavy for even two husky men that they didn't spare a casual glance at their tires, and they showed no surprise that the back of the truck sank under its weight. They went back for the toaster oven and radio, which they took into the cab with them. On the way, the axeman stepped over Sam. Tripping him didn't seem like a good idea.

The axeman turned and looked at Sam, gloating. He picked up his axe from the truck. "Now, you noisy little rat, it's your turn," he said. He raised the axe.

Sam gasped, "Don't, please don't!" The axe flashed through the air. Sam cringed and strained at his rope. Suddenly he was rolling into a gooseberry bush, the loose end of the rope snapping at him.

The axeman laughed. "You keep your mouth shut, or next time you'll get a taste of the real thing." He swung into the driver's seat.

As the ignition was switched on, Sam's heart beat faster again. How soon would they notice?

The truck bumped horribly going down the hill, but over so many rocks it wouldn't surprise them. They didn't turn on their headlights.

The truck turned onto the road and disappeared slowly into the trees. Then it stopped, with the motor still running, and Sam heard a door open.

That seemed like a very good time to make himself scarce. With his hands still tied, he struggled to his feet and ran up the hill, heading for the thickest bush he could find. But he had never realized how hard it was to run without arms to balance you. And the loose end of the rope kept catching on branches.

The roar lifted off the top of Kate's head and poured ice cubes down her spine. It did the same to Tweed, judging from the tremor in his cheek as she lifted the bit into his mouth. If only she could make those creatures leave her little brother alone. But she knew she was no match for two of them. And Sam wasn't calling her name. The best she could do would be to get help as fast as possible.

She led Tweed through the gate to the half-buried mound of ancient farm machinery that was their mounting block, and in a moment she had scrambled onto his back. Pointing Tweed in the general direction of the road, she drove her legs into him.

Tweed threw up his head in astonishment. Why had Kate suddenly taken to steering for herself? Why did she demand speed in the middle of the night? And what on earth was the matter with Sam?

But the noble Lord Tweedsmuir did as he was asked without waiting for explanations. He trotted silently through the grass till he came to the road.

As soon as she heard gravel under them, Kate turned him left, away from the house. She wished she could ride him on the grass shoulder where no one could hear their hoofbeats, but then they might stray into the swamp. The road offered the safest way to put distance behind them. Tweed trotted confidently forward, and when she drew her leg back and urged him still harder, he went up into a canter.

Fine, thought Kate, so where are we heading? To phone the police? Well, we won't come to a house with a working phone until we're past the fallen telephone pole. If this were the city there would be a phone crew working on it, but it will probably be days before they get around to our neck of the woods. So we're galloping right into a great mess of wires and pole. Will it electrocute us? Hydro lines would for sure — and for all I know, the hydro may be down as well. I don't know if Sam tried to turn the lights on. Tweed, I hope you know an electrical hazard when you see it.

She gave him a completely loose rein so he could choose his own way, and she anchored both hands in his mane. Her ears strained for the sound of someone chasing her. The wind whistled in her ears, and the woods were full of a hundred little noises, any of which might turn into wheels roaring up from behind.

The yells stopped short. What had they done to

Sam to shut him up? Stories of children who disappeared without a trace floated up from the dark backwaters of her memory.

Why, oh why had they gone ahead with this camping scheme that had sent both parents away from them?

Tweed slowed to a walk, then halted. She squeezed him on. Hesitantly, he turned to the left and stretched out his neck as if peering at something. Then she was pitched backwards onto his loins and felt him picking his way over very uneven ground. A branch brushed her face. She went cold with fear. But if she tried to steer him she might get them into even worse trouble. He paused, then jumped down a bank, throwing Kate into the air like a kangaroo — luckily a kangaroo with paws firmly fixed in his mane.

When she found her seat again, they were walking on gravel. There was no way of telling if they had skirted the fallen pole or simply turned around so they were now heading for home — and the thieves' waiting arms.

"Where are you taking us, Tweed?" she whispered.

He was trotting with his long explorer's stride, his head raised to see what lay round the next corner. When he went toward home, his neck stretched long and low.

Sooner or later, she would have to look for a house. How on earth was she going to do that? This wasn't a city neighbourhood where TVs blared late movies. The two or three houses along this end of the road would be silent as log piles, and Kate would never know when she was passing them.

If she kept on, in the end she would reach the highway and hear pavement underfoot. The thought of speeding cars scared her, but maybe she could flag one down before it ran into her.

Help had to come soon, though. The sound of that axe splintering the door rang in her ears, with Sam's last scream. Summoning her courage, Kate shouted, "Help!"

There was no answer except the faintest of echoes among the rustling leaves.

She shouted every ten strides. She felt foolish in her lacy pyjamas and bare feet, shouting to the empty woods, the deserted weekend cottages, the dangerous strangers. She was just as likely to meet with friends of the burglars as anyone who would help them.

At the twenty-seventh "Help!" a dog barked — an angry dog with a big voice, who quickly worked himself into a fury. Was he running to attack them? Kate pulled Tweed back. There was a metallic clash, then a boom like a small tree falling. The dog bayed like a maniac, but it came no nearer. The clash might have been the dog hitting the end of its chain.

Not wanting to risk tangling with either the chain or the dog, Kate stayed still and yelled for help at the top of her voice, an octave higher than the dog's. Their duet did not please Tweed, who fidgeted and tried to turn away. But she turned his head firmly toward the dog. After a tense moment, an aluminum door opened.

"What is it?" asked a sleepy and irritated man.

"Some men have broken into our house. Would you phone the police for me — if your phone is working?"

"Oh. You live at the old Pippard place, don't you?" asked the man in a less unfriendly voice, though he still sounded half asleep. She had no idea who he was, but it wasn't surprising that people recognized them as the new family on the road. "Shut up, Brandy," he said, and the dog's voice sank to a growl. "Sure, come on in and use the phone."

"Would you mind doing it for me, please? I'm blind."

"What's that?" The man didn't believe her — blind people don't ride horses. So he wouldn't believe her about the burglars, either. Unless he was one himself.

But she couldn't afford not to trust him. She tried a new tack. "Would you please help me get my horse past your dog? He's very quiet with people, but he's not used to dogs."

"Oh. Okay." The door banged shut and bedroom slippers shuffled their way down a gravel drive.

Kate explained. "Two men came in a truck and broke down our door with an axe. I got away, but they caught my younger brother."

"Really? What did they do to him?" asked the man. He sounded close and not dangerous, so Kate slid down and held out the reins.

"I don't know," she answered, not quite managing to keep her voice from cracking.

The reins were taken from her hands, and she stepped back and laid her hand on Tweed's croup. She followed as he was led a little distance uphill and halted. "The phone is straight through in the kitchen," said the man helpfully. "The Perth police number is taped to the wall."

"I can't leave my horse. *Please* would you call? And tell them there's a telephone pole down across Waddle Creek Road, so they have to go round by Lammermoor. And to hurry!"

"It's all right, I've got them," called a woman's voice from the house. "Hello, we have an armed robbery and assault in progress, would you send a cruiser right away . . ."

A few minutes later, the receiver clicked and the woman came to the door. "They're on their way. Come in and have a cup of tea. Don will look after your horse, he likes them. You really are blind, aren't you? Where are your parents?"

Kate choked down a sob. Help was halfway there — it was a great relief, yet it wasn't enough, not nearly. "My mother will be coming home and run right into the robbers. I need to call my Dad to stop her."

The woman took her into the kitchen and dialled for her. After five agonizing rings, Dad answered, and Kate poured out the tale.

"But your mother left here a quarter of an hour ago," he said.

"Oh no, she'll run slap into them. And they have an axe. Can't you stop her?"

"But I haven't got the car. And Cynthia sure

won't lend me hers again. My goose is cooked there."

Kate choked. A car was supposed to be standard equipment for fathers, but of course he didn't have one now. How could she forget? Two eyes, two women, no car, no help in an emergency, that was her father. The tears welled up in her eyes, and she held the phone away from her face so he wouldn't hear her sob.

Perhaps he did, though. After a long minute of silence, he said in a different, deeper voice, "Look, stay where you are, Katkin. Don't worry, I'll get there somehow, even if I have to charter a helicopter."

"Don't do that. Tweed *hates* helicopters," sobbed Kate.

The axeman ran up the hill roaring, "You lousy rat, I'll skin you alive!" His heavy tread rocked the cabin floor as he strode straight through and out the other side.

Sam, cowering in the middle of a cedar with twigs digging into every bit of him, didn't dare breathe.

A flashlight played over the trees. "Come out of there, if you know what's good for you!" snarled the voice.

For once, Sam longed to be shorter and thinner so he could disappear behind a tree trunk. The blood rushed in his ears. He shut his eyes tight so they wouldn't catch the light and betray him.

Cursing, the man ran down the hill again. The

truck moved on slowly. Before it passed out of hearing, it stopped again.

Perhaps they had pulled in somewhere to change the tire. It would only take one of them: the other could do what he liked with the axe. Sam strained his ears for the sounds of a thief creeping back to lie in wait for him.

He wondered how Kate was managing. Likely she'd fallen into the swamp, and if he ever escaped he'd have to go looking for her. Not with the burglars around, though. Suppose they followed him and caught both of them?

A long, anxious time later, an engine came roaring up the road. It didn't sound like the truck. Could it be Mum coming back? He'd better run down and get her to drive him away, and they could look for Kate. But suppose it was only more burglars? Cautiously he worked his way half out of the tree and threaded his legs through his tied hands.

Red lights flashed and a sleek police cruiser pulled up. Two uniformed giants got out carrying a high-powered lantern.

Sam ran out and caught up with them at the cabin. They looked from the broken door to his bound wrists. "Someone called about a break-in," said one officer.

"The burglars are up the road somewhere changing a flat tire," blurted Sam. "They must have hidden in the trees. If we hurry we'll catch them."

The officers strode quickly down the hill. As they went, Sam heard the truck start up in the distance. "That's them!" he shouted.

The policemen ran to their cruiser and drew Sam into the front seat between them. They set off with siren screaming. A rabbit leaped out of their road, trees rushed by in a blur. Before long they picked up the blacked-out truck in their headlights. It was bucketing along at high speed on four good tires. Apparently the burglars were more efficient than Dad at changing wheels. It was no match for the cruiser, though. Where the road turned south to Lammermoor, the cruiser pulled ahead on the inside and forced the truck to screech to a halt.

The police driver picked up his radio phone and reported to headquarters. Sam felt as if he had stepped into a TV movie. The men got out of their truck when ordered to, but they looked murderous and admitted nothing. They demanded to see a lawyer.

The police asked Sam to get out of the cruiser to identify the men as the ones who had threatened him with an axe and tied him up. One of the officers copied down what he said, and examined the rope around his hands before starting to cut it carefully away.

In his clammy pyjamas, Sam began to shiver. The gravel road hurt his bare feet. He would have liked to wrap himself up in a blanket in the back seat. He wondered if he would have to sit with the burglars on the way to the police station. Suppose they took him hostage and hijacked the cruiser?

Right into the middle of the scene drove Sam's mother. She slowed down to stare; Sam saw her puzzled face reflecting the cruiser's flashing red lights. Then she made as if to drive on. Sam yelled, "Mum! Wait up!"

She slammed on the brakes. "Sam! What have you done?"

Now and then, when he kicked the walls, she had called him a delinquent, but until that moment he had never thought she really believed the law would catch up with him. Just because it looked as if a policeman was handcuffing him, was that any reason to suppose he'd been arrested? "I've foiled a burglary," he protested.

"Where's Kate?" she asked urgently.

"I don't know."

"What? Where did you see her last?"

"She rode off on Tweed to get help."

"Oh no!" Mum's eyes grew big with horror.

A policeman came after Mum for her name, address, and date of birth. She kept asking about Kate, but they had no answers. They took her to identify the things in the truck, and she grew angrier than Sam had ever seen her. She turned on the axeman and shouted, "Tell me what you've done to my daughter or you'll be sorry you were ever born!"

Just then another long, low car drove up. The woods were becoming as crowded as a movie set. Sam thought this was another police cruiser, until he saw the taxi sign. Then he knew at last that he was dreaming, because no taxi had ever muddied its wheels on Waddle Creek Road.

Out jumped his father. He grabbed Mum in one arm and Sam in the other and cried, "Are you all right?"

Mum shouted, "Those crooks ripped out our stove, and nobody will tell me what they've done to Kate."

"She's all right, she's at a house up the road, I've spoken to her," said Dad, hugging them tight. "She sent me here to warn you."

Like a rigid, vacuum-sealed package when you slit it and the air rushes in and it goes soft, Sam's mother went limp with relief. She folded her arms around Sam and his father, and nuzzled her head between their two necks, and said, "Thank God." She showered them both with kisses. Sam was so relieved himself that he kissed her back, even though all the men were watching.

Later, two policemen, two parents, and a taxi driver listened with wide-open ears as Sam told the full story of the burglary. The police complimented him on his neat work in flattening the tire, which had allowed them to catch the thieves red-handed. What impressed Mum and Dad most, though, was how he had covered Kate's getaway completely by yelling. They had always said his voice was loud enough to deafen a person. For once, that had come in really useful.

Kate was sitting on a lawn chair with a blanket wrapped around her, holding a mug of tea in one hand and Tweed's reins in the other while he grazed the lawn. She didn't much like tea, but the mug warmed her hand and the steam rose agreeably to her chin. From the doorstep, Mrs. Thurlow was telling her about Brandy and how he was really friendly except that when he was chained up at night he knew it was his job to scare strangers away.

As if to demonstrate, Brandy began barking furiously, ran out to the end of his chain, and boomed his doghouse. From this angle, it sounded more like a practised routine than a fit of stark fury. But the stranger's voice sounded wary as he said, "Can you tell me where . . . Oh, Kate!"

"Dad, you made it! Where's the helicopter?"

"Oh, you know me, I always travel on foot."

When he had answered all her questions about Sam and Mum and they had thanked the Thurlows, he gave her a leg up on Tweed and led her homeward. He said, "The cabin isn't fit to live in now, but we'll finish the night there, and tomorrow we'll all go back to my place and phone up a carpenter."

"But what about Tweed?" asked his owner.

"We'll call the Bensons in the morning."

Kate's heart sank. She might have known they wouldn't let her keep him in the end. Her father must be tired of walking the back roads beside a horse. She could hear him limping, and there was a hurting edge in his voice. They had tried to show him they were growing up into responsible young people who would be all fun and no hassle, but instead they had got into really serious trouble and dragged him out in the middle of the night to rescue them. He would crawl back into his trouble-free apartment and not want to know about them.

"Tell me, how did you find your way around the

fallen wires?" he asked. "The road is completely blocked."

"Tweed figured it out. He's smarter than your average bicycle, you know."

"He sure is. If you hadn't gone for help with him, the burglars would have got away with everything. We're lucky to have such a horse to look after us." He slapped Tweed's neck.

Kate sat up. "You mean it? That we're lucky to have him? And you mean the 'us', too?"

"Yes, I mean the 'us' most of all. When I got back to the apartment, it seemed so empty and lonely. Cynthia came in — walked straight in without knocking, and I asked her to go away because I was feeling terrible. She wouldn't go. She started to make an ugly scene about my weekend with you, so I had to throw her out. And I was sitting there, thinking what a wonderful time we'd had up here together and how stupid I'd been to let you all slip away from me, when your call came. I realized that if anything happened to you guys I couldn't go on living. So just now, I asked your mother if she'd let me have another chance."

"What did she say?"

"That it might save her having to drive me home so often."

Kate laughed. Her mother had said she despised him because he ran away. But he had lasted out the whole journey and he had come racing back when he was needed. "We could always build the cabin bigger," said Kate.

"But Kate, is that really all right with you?

Because you're the one who has the most to forgive. You've had so much to cope with and all I've done is make it harder. I can't tell you how sorry I am. It was because feeling so helpless frightened me, but I couldn't admit to being a coward, not even to myself. And it isn't even that I've got braver now. But you've faced everything with such courage all along — my leaving, the move, your interfering grandparents, the horse, the camping trip, and now the break-in. So now I see there's nothing to be afraid of. And I love you, Kate. Please will you take me back?"

Kate stretched out her hand and found a wiry, tight-curled beard. She leaned forward and planted a kiss on the cheek above it. "Of course," she said.

When Sam came downstairs next morning, he found two sleeping parents entwined in front of the open doorway, living proof that you never know what will come in when your door is broken down.

Next weekend they made a big bonfire at the top of the hill with the broken bits of door, and into the middle they thrust the separation agreement. Dad gave a running commentary for Kate as a black shadow crept up it, followed by a blue flame that turned gold, then white. Kate listened to the merry crackling and led three rousing cheers.

They roasted marshmallows over the bonfire, and gave Tweed his full share.